A Home Subscription! It's the easiest and most convenient way to get every one of the exciting Coventry Romance Novels! ...And you get 4 of them FREE!

You pay nothing extra for this convenience: there are no additional charges...you don't even pay for postage! Fill out and send us the handy coupon now, and we'll send you 4 exciting Coventry Romance novels absolutely FREE!

SEND NO MONEY, GET THESE
FOUR BOOKS FREE!

- -

C1081

MAIL THIS COUPON TODAY TO:
**COVENTRY HOME
SUBSCRIPTION SERVICE
6 COMMERCIAL STREET
HICKSVILLE, NEW YORK 11801**

YES, please start a Coventry Romance Home Subscription in my name, and send me FREE and without obligation to buy, my 4 Coventry Romances. If you do not hear from me after I have examined my 4 FREE books, please send me the 6 new Coventry Romances each month as soon as they come off the presses. I understand that I will be billed only $9.00 for all 6 books. There are no shipping and handling nor any other hidden charges. There is no minimum number of monthly purchases that I have to make. In fact, I can cancel my subscription at any time. The first 4 FREE books are mine to keep as a gift, even if I do not buy any additional books.

For added convenience, your monthly subscription may be charged automatically to your credit card:

☐ Master Charge **42101**   ☐ Visa **42101**

Credit Card #_____

Expiration Date_____

Name_____
(Please Print)

Address_____

City_____State_____Zip_____

Signature_____

☐ Bill Me Direct Each Month **40105**

Publisher reserves the right to substitute alternate FREE books. Sales tax collected where required by law. Offer valid for new members only.
Allow 3-4 weeks for delivery. Prices subject to change without notice.

MY LORDS, LADIES
AND MARJORIE

by

Marion Chesney

FAWCETT COVENTRY • NEW YORK

MY LORDS, LADIES AND MARJORIE

Published by Fawcett Coventry Books, a unit of CBS
Publications, the Consumer Publishing Division of CBS Inc.

ISBN: 0-449-50216-3

Printed in the United States of America

First Fawcett Coventry printing: October 1981

10 9 8 7 6 5 4 3 2 1

For Harry Scott Gibbons
and Charles David Bravos Gibbons
With love

Chapter One

"Life is a backwater," said Miss Marjorie Montmorency-James to the looking glass. She practiced a soulful look and hoped she looked like that famous actress, Ellen Terry.

"Life is a backwater," she said again, but, since she was alone in the drawing room, no one replied and, when she turned around, there was no one to look back at her except a multitude of paper eyes in the photographs stacked on top of the Bechstein grand piano. Marjorie sank down disconsolately into the red plush upholstery of a carved walnut chair and stared at the toes of her pointed openwork shoes.

The house was very still and silent. But then her grandmother's well-run house always was, protected from the noisy elements of the world outside by thick carpets and thick curtains. The well-trained servants were about their duties in the kitchen. Although Marjorie often wondered idly what it would be like to be a servant and live one's days out in a basement under gaslight, she had never gone into the kitchens although she had lived her eighteen years in this house on Haddon Common in London.

Neither had she penetrated to the attics, only being dimly aware that they existed when the servants' alarm clock sometimes disturbed her sleep.

She had been brought up by her grandmother, Mrs. Wilton. Her parents had died in a carriage accident when she was only a baby. Mrs. Wilton did not believe in sending a young girl to school and so she had been educated at home by a governess, only recently dismissed. Marjorie was lonely but she did not miss her governess who had been a strange, quiet, timid female called Miss Muggles. Marjorie was relieved to find that Miss Muggles had found other employment but, apart from that, thought of her hardly at all.

She lived her young days out in the house on Haddon Common—a square white house, rather like a bathing lido, designed in the late 1880s by a Scottish architect and considered then to be the height of modernity.

Haddon Common was a trim square of green

surrounded by large houses and villas. It was strictly aging middle class. No aristocrat took up residence to flutter the breasts of the elderly widows who made up the neighborhood. No vulgar poor ventured on the sedate common or the tree-lined streets to remind them of the less fortunate.

Social outings were confined to church on Sunday—Anglican of course and *very* High—bridge parties with her grandmother's elderly friends and knitting socks for the Underprivileged at a weekly sewing bee. Marjorie's sole hobby was that of buying picture postcards of famous beauties—like Ellen Terry—and trying to change her face and expression to that of the dewy-eyed belles.

Marjorie was quite beautiful but there was no one to tell her so. Her grandmother's highest compliment was that Marjorie looked "very well."

She had soft hair of the nut-brown variety that was so fashionable. Blondes and redheads were considered "unfortunate." She had a clear pale skin and very large gray eyes which changed like water on a winter's day, sometimes looking black and sometimes silver.

On this day that was to change her life, Marjorie was wearing a high-collared blouse with a deep blond lace bertha falling over her well-shaped bosom. In contrast, her long alpaca skirt was severely tailored. Although she had not formally been "out" anywhere, she wore her hair up.

It had been raining heavily all morning, drenching, soaking spring rain. Now toward evening, the rain had ceased and a pale, watery sunlight, low in the horizon, was gilding the laurel bushes in the front garden.

The drawing room suddenly seemed close and stuffy. Marjorie rose to her feet and walked from the drawing room, through the dark hall, harlequined with diamonds of light from the stained glass on the door, and out into the garden.

A light warm breeze had sprung up bringing with it the promise of winter's end. The still bare branches of the lilac trees near the wrought iron gates made a lacy pattern against the pale, newly washed sky.

"Life is a backwater," said Marjorie for the third time. But this time she said it bitterly. She was overcome by a longing for excitement, for love, for flirtation, for theaters, for restaurants, for the company of young men. The air was full of promises of youth and excitement—promises carried to every young girl in London except Marjorie. Grannie's weekly social evening was the only thing on her dull horizon.

Marjorie had once been in love—at the age of fourteen. She had fallen madly for the red-haired butcher's boy and used to wait with shaking coltish legs at the tradesmen's entrance for his arrival with the weekly joint. She had weaved fantasies about him, fought for him, nursed him through various deadly and fictitious diseases.

And then one day she had overheard him laughing about her with Rose, the pretty parlormaid. "Fair smitten, she is," he had jeered. Marjorie's heart had died of humiliation. For weeks she had planned exotic revenges. She would ride her milk-white steed across the common and spurn his grubby peasant soul beneath her silver hoofs. But Marjorie could not even ride. The butcher's boy left for another part of London. The hurt disappeared.

But now as she breathed in the smell of damp grass and dripping evergreens, the memory of those first tremulous, passionate emotions came back to her vividly. She stretched her arms up high to the darkening sky and then dropped them helplessly to her sides.

A shaft of white light struck across the lawn. Rose had turned up the gaslight to prepare the drawing room for grandmother's evening social. Already in her mind's eye, Marjorie could smell the camphor and cologne of the old ladies and hear their frail, tired voices. She sighed. The breeze had turned chilly and damp, fluttering the lace of her blouse and raising the soft strands of hair from her forehead.

"I want *him*," said Marjorie fiercely. But she did not yet know who he was or who he might be, that shadowy lover. The lights of her grandmother's rented carriage bobbed to a halt outside the gates.

Suddenly cold, Marjorie did not wait to greet her grandmother but turned on her little high heels and pattered over the gravel of the drive, back into the warmth and silence of the house.

There were three old ladies in the drawing room that evening when Marjorie reluctantly entered—and a newcomer.

At first she did not see the newcomer, her bored eyes ranging from the familiar sight of old Mrs. Jenkins mumbling meringues, old Mrs. Bassett slurping tea with little finger sticking rigidly out, and old Mrs. Fyfe-Bartholomew dozing in front of the fire. Then she noticed the strange lady. She was very tall and dramatic looking. Although she must have been in her forties, she carried herself with the youthful assurance of a young girl. She wore a large velour hat impaled with a long pheasant's tail feather. Her eyes were dark and liquid and slightly bulging and her rouged mouth was drawn into a permanent pout. She was dressed from head to foot in black velvet and long ropes of black jet beads swung from her long neck.

"My granddaughter," Mrs. Wilton was saying as Marjorie moved forward. "Marjorie, may I present a newcomer to our little community, Lady Bethons.

Marjorie curtsied low. She had been about to dismiss the newcomer in her mind as someone of no great moment, but . . . a lady! A real, live aristocrat. Lady Bethons held out a beringed glove in a swanlike motion and Marjorie, who did not know it was very vulgar indeed to wear your rings over your gloves, was entranced.

"My lady," she breathed, while her mind raced. Perhaps Lady Bethons had a son? Of course, she had. A dashing young man with fine aristocratic features who would fall in love with Marjorie and would sweep her off to his palace in the country. She could almost see herself pouring tea for King Edward. You must not blame Marjorie for being a snob. Everyone was. It was the nature of our times.

"Ah, my dear child," said Lady Bethons, drawing back and raising her gloved hands as if to frame a picture. "Beautiful, quite beautiful. Absolutely Burne-Jones, my dear. Have you got a fellah?"

Marjorie assumed a world-weary air. "There are no young gentlemen around here, my lady." How thrilling to say "my lady" to a guest in one's own drawing room!

"Poor child!" exclaimed Lady Bethons. She opened her reticule and drew out a slim gold case and a long cigarette holder. Under Marjorie's fascinated eyes, she extracted a cigarette from the case, fitted it into the holder, lit the cigarette with a Swan Vesta and puffed a delicate cloud of blue smoke across the room.

"I adore young men," she went on. "I love to have them sit at my feet."

"Don't we all," fluted Mrs. Jenkins from under the shadow of an enormous hat laden with wax fruit. "But we're all too old. No young men want to sit at the feet of a lot of old hens like us."

"S'right," came the strangely underwater voice of old Mrs. Bassett, although, in fact, it was, so to speak, under tea since she hardly ever lifted her face from her teacup. Mrs. Fyfe-Bartholomew snored.

For one moment, Lady Bethons's eyes flashed and her restless hands with their weight of glittering rings moved briefly toward the large steel hatpin in her hat as if she would pluck it out and stab it right through the whalebone barrier of Mrs. Jenkins's corsets to the old wrinkled bosom underneath and thence to her vulgar middle-class heart. Marjorie suffered with her. Suffered intensely as she blushed for her grandmother's common guests. How this fine aristocratic soul must feel soiled by their very presence.

Mrs. Wilton, Marjorie's grandmother, moved forward to take her place at the tea tray. Mrs. Jenkins immediately engaged her in conversation. The new vicar had said a very puzzling thing in his sermon . . .

"Oh, I have no secrets," said Marjorie, in answer to a question put to her by the dazzling visitor.

"All gels have," insisted Lady Bethons. "Tell me, *do*. There must be some young man." Marjorie thought of the butcher's boy and blushed.

"Aha!" cried Lady Bethons, tossing her head back in a gay laugh. "I thought as much. But I will not tease. When do you come out?"

"I don't," confessed Marjorie. "Not in London, I mean. But in the summer, we go to Sandypoint and they have a few balls there and grandmama says I may attend."

"Sandypoint!" exclaimed Lady Bethons in accents of loathing.

"Darling child! You must have a London Season. The balls, the parties, the young gallants. Why, I remember when Bertie, the Prince of Wales he was then . . . but you must not tell a *soul* . . ."

"Oh, no," gasped Marjorie, feeling quite dizzy at the mention of this royal name.

"Well, Bertie," said Lady Bethons, lowering her voice to a deep contralto, "said to me at the Duchess of Codlingham's ball, 'Felicity,' he said, *pressing my hand,* 'were it not for my royal destiny, I would marry *you.*' "

"Ooooh!" cried Marjorie, clasping her hands.

"But you did marry someone else . . . someone you loved."

"Ah, yes. I married poor Jimmy. So dashing, so gallant. He died . . . bravely."

"May I ask how . . . I mean if it does not distress you," ventured Marjorie, her expressive eyes turning almost black with interest.

"It was a long time ago. He died under the hot Indian sun. Some foul native stabbed him. He rolled to the sand. The sun burned down on his face. 'Felicity,' he cried. 'I love you . . . madly'. But there was no one there to hear. And so he perished."

"If there was no one there to hear," pointed out Marjorie timidly, "then how did you come to learn of his last words?"

Lady Bethons's eyes took on a strange, fixed expression for a moment, and then she said hurriedly, "I meant no one of *consequence*. His native bearer told his colonel of Jimmy's last moments before the poor brute died himself. But I should not be distressing a young girl like you with such sad stories. Ah, I see the card table is being set up. You play?"

"Sometimes." Marjorie was disappointed at this break in the conversation. "But I am not very good."

But Lady Bethons had left her, in spirit anyway, as her eyes fastened on the green baize table that the parlormaid was erecting in front of the fire.

Marjorie waited impatiently for the games

of cards to finish so that she could engage the fascinating Lady Bethons in conversation again.

But no sooner were the hands of bridge finished than Lady Bethons took her leave. Mrs. Jenkins had won, and won heavily, and Lady Bethons did not look at all pleased.

Marjorie waited until she was alone with her grandmother. "Grandmama . . . ," she began.

Mrs. Wilton looked at her curiously. "You always call me 'grannie,' " she said.

"Never mind," said Marjorie in a rush. "I have had such an exciting evening. A real, live lady! And she knows King Edward . . . or rather she knew him when he was the Prince of Wales and . . . and . . . she calls him 'Bertie' and he wanted to marry her." Marjorie did not feel disloyal to Lady Bethons by telling her grandmother.

Mrs. Wilton watched with some amusement as Marjorie's mouth puckered up in a fair imitation of Lady Bethons and she tossed her head back in the same manner.

"And you would never let me wear rings over my gloves," went on Marjorie, sinking her voice to imitate Lady Bethons's contralto.

"No. It's common," said Mrs. Wilton.

Mrs. Wilton was a small, birdlike woman of seventy with little plump hands and feet. She had hooded eyes and a small hooked nose and in her red velvet evening gown she looked remarkably like a Christmas robin.

"Felicity Bethons was on the stage before she married the East End scrap dealer, Jimmy Simons," said Mrs. Wilton. "She used to be quite beautiful, you know, in a flashy sort of way."

"On the stage! An actress!" cried Marjorie.

"Well, no, front row of the chorus in Falk's Follies."

"But ... you said 'Jimmy Simons' not Jimmy Bethons."

"Jimmy Simons made a fortune out of his scrap dealing and bought himself a knighthood and changed his name to Bethons. Sir Jimmy Bethons, he became. It must have cost him a mint."

"And he died in India?" queried Marjorie, faint but pursuing.

"No, no, dear. Not India. The East India dock. He was watching the ships and had a stroke. One of the lascars ran for help but he had died instantly."

"Was it a hot day?" asked Marjorie, reluctant to relinquish the picture of soldier Jimmy under the burning sun.

Mrs. Wilton looked at her curiously. "I don't know, my dear. What has old Felicity been telling you? She always was a silly thing. She certainly wouldn't have met King Edward when he was Prince of Wales. She probably saw him when Jimmy was knighted but as for His Majesty wishing to *marry* her . . ."

Marjorie sighed and stared at her hands. Haddon Common had swirled around in a delicious rainbow of aristocratic enchantment for one whole evening. "How do you know so much about Lady Bethons?" she asked at last.

"Mrs. Jenkins's lady's maid is a former theatrical dresser and she told Mrs. Jenkins, who told me."

"Servants' gossip!" cried Marjorie, her eyes flashing. "It could all be untrue."

"Lady Bethons smells of the shop and of greasepaint," said her grandmother tartly, "and I would not have her in my house except for the fact that she plays a fine hand of bridge. I'm sorry to disappoint you, Marjorie. But at least I shall not have to live with the image of Lady Bethons during the next few weeks. The minute you admire someone, you try to change your personality to theirs. I sometimes wish you could go on the stage and get it out of your system. The fact is, Marjorie, you lead too dull a life for a girl of your years. Perhaps I shall do something about it. But not tonight, my dear. A most exhausting evening. And sometimes Mrs. Jenkins is really *too* lucky. Some evenings, she seems to win every game. Turn out the gas before you go to bed, Marjorie, and put the guard in front of the fire."

Marjorie dutifully pecked her grandmother on the cheek and waited until her small figure had left the room. Then she plumped down on an overstuffed sofa with a sigh. Somehow the boredom of her existence seemed even more unbearable after even that one taste of pinchbeck aristocracy.

She felt too restless to follow her grandmother up to bed. Some illustrated papers were lying piled neatly on an occasional table beside the sofa. She picked up a copy of the *Tatler* and idly turned the pages. Most of the subjects in the photographs looked as if they had been stuffed and mounted especially for the photographer as their eyes stared glassily up at her.

Then she came to one large one that had more animation than the others and, all of a sudden, her eyes were riveted to the page. There was a group of bright young things in the act of playing croquet on the lawn of a country house. In the foreground of the picture was a tall man who had turned to stare at the photographer. It was a hard, haughty, arrogant face with a proud nose, a firm mouth and a strong chin. Hair that looked black sprang away from a high broad forehead. The eyes were large and fine and well-shaped and seemed to stare straight at the mesmerized Marjorie in disdainful surprise.

And Marjorie fell in love in that instant.

Rapidly she read the caption. "On the right"—
ah, that was he!—"Lord Philip Cavendish."

"I must meet him, somehow," thought
Marjorie desperately. "If only I were a titled
lady or an American heiress."

She slowly looked round the luxurious
drawing room. Her grandmother was a very
rich woman. Was there any reason then why
she, Marjorie, should not have a Season? Just
one Season?

Then Marjorie's expressive mouth drooped.
She was middle class. Mrs. Wilton's money
had been left her by her late husband who
had owned a chain of grocers' shops. There
was no way to lose the stigma of trade. Even
Mrs. Wilton herself spoke jeeringly of people
who "smelled of the shop."

Marjorie had never questioned her grandmother on the subject but she felt sure that
Mrs. Wilton, like everyone else in Haddon
Common, believed that your station in life
had been appointed by God and it would be
flying in the face of heavenly law and order
to try to step out of it.

"I shall ask her in the morning," thought
Marjorie, still clutching the magazine. "She
can only say no."

Which is what Mrs Wilton did . . . a flat,
unequivocal "NO."

"If I stay here in Haddon Common, I may
meet unsuitable young men," pointed out
Marjorie desperately.

"Nonsense," said Mrs. Wilton. "There are no young men in Haddon Common, unsuitable or otherwise."

Marjorie bent her head over her congealing breakfast. "Then I shall find one," she thought. "Just you wait and see."

Chapter Two

Mrs. Wilton's first small attempt to divert Marjorie's mind from thoughts of a London Season was to buy her a dog. It was a small Scotch terrier called Mackintosh and had Marjorie not become obsessed with that black-and-white picture of Lord Philip Cavendish, she would have been delighted with the animal.

As it was, she enjoyed the stocky little dog's company in a lukewarm way, made sure it was exercised and fed and its rough coat brushed. The animal also made a tolerably good confidant and learned along with Marjorie as she pored over a large volume of Burke's *Peerage* that Lord Philip was the youngest son of the Duke of Dunster. This exalted fact should have poured cold water on the ambitions of any sensible girl but Marjorie had not been much in the way of experiencing the realities of life, immured as she was in the genteel backwater of Haddon Common, and so everything seemed possible and, in her nightly dreams, she walked and talked with Lord Philip.

She had not, however, forgotten her resolve to find an unsuitable man. Her grandmother might grant her a Season if it meant removing her from the evil influence of unsuitable company.

At last she found him.

Mrs. Wilton became aware that there was some strange influence in Marjorie's life. One day she came across Marjorie kneeling in prayer over a rosary. Mrs. Wilton had smiled tolerantly at that, assuming that Marjorie had read some ridiculous novel about a nun and was bent as usual on emulating the heroine.

Then a crucifix appeared above Marjorie's bed. That gave Mrs. Wilton a few anxious moments but she decided not to mention it.

Then the blow fell. She was entertaining her elderly friends and the vulgar Lady Bethons to tea when Mrs. Jenkins put her cup down in her saucer with a smart click and pointed to the far wall of the drawing room.

"Dear me, Mrs. Wilton," said Mrs. Jenkins, aghast. "Not turning papist are we?"

Mrs. Wilton slowly turned round. There in a corner of the drawing room under the English landscapes and hunting prints was a picture of the virgin and child framed neatly in black passe-partout. Not by one of the masters either. One of those cheap, highly colored religious paintings.

"I don't know how on earth that got there," she said, urgently ringing the bell.

When Rose entered, Mrs. Wilton waved at the picture. "Who put that thing there, Rose?"

"Miss Marjorie, ma'am," said Rose with the shining bright look of restrained glee a good servant adopts when he or she knows that one of the betters is going to cop it.

"Nonsense!" began Mrs. Wilton, and then she remembered the crucifix and the rosary. "I admit Marjorie *has* been acting strangely. Have you any idea who might be responsible for Marjorie's . . . er . . . Romish behavior? Speak up, Rose. Some lady from St. Mary's congregation, perhaps?"

"I think, ma'am," said Rose, enjoying herself hugely, "that if you look out of the window you'll see Miss Marjorie on the common with a certain gentleman."

"Don't be so coy and secretive, Rose," snapped Mrs. Wilton. "When I ask you a simple question, I expect a direct answer." But gasps from the window as her friends stared out and a high sniggering laugh from Lady Bethons forced her to leave Rose and follow suit. The company parted to allow her a full view.

There in the middle of Haddon Common stood Marjorie. She had Mackintosh on a leash. The spring day was fine and she was wearing a straw boater, a striped shirt-blouse and a white linen skirt.

And she was smiling gaily up into the face of a very handsome young priest who seemed equally enchanted with Marjorie's company. He had a square tanned face and very white teeth and a shock of blond hair. In all, he was certainly much too good-looking to be a priest.

"Oh, dear," gasped Mrs. Wilton. "Who on earth is he?"

"Oh, that's Father Benjamin from St. Mary's," drawled Lady Bethons, enjoying herself hugely. "All the young girls are mad about him but Marjorie is the only one he seems interested in."

"Dear me!" wailed Mrs. Wilton. "A Roman Catholic priest. Oh, the shame of it! And Marjorie such a good Anglican. I shall speak to his religious superior. What will our good vicar say? Marjorie will be ruined. I know Marjorie! She'll fall into a religious fever and become a nun! Oh, dear! What am I to do?"

"Take her away from Haddon Common," said Lady Bethons, lowering her voice dramatically. "He is a new priest, you know, and perhaps it is part of some devilish plot on the part of the Church of Rome. They plan to lure our young girls away by seducing their minds."

"It's not her mind I'm worried about," snapped Mrs. Wilton.

"Piffle," said old Mrs. Bassett. "Absolute balderdash! You're all takin' it too seriously. Call the gel in and have a word with her."

Mrs. Wilton flapped a hand at Rose who scampered out and shortly afterward could be seen heading across the common in Marjorie's direction.

There was a heavy silence in the drawing room. The old grandfather clock ticked away in the corner, a log fell in the grate and the bright sunlight flickered through the bushes and trees of the garden to waver over the rose-patterned wallpaper and carved walnut furniture.

Then Marjorie came in with Mackintosh at her heels. She stood in the doorway with her hands clasped as if in prayer and her eyes turned up toward the ceiling.

Mrs. Wilton sighed.

"Marjorie!" she said crossly. "What on earth are you doing talking to a Catholic priest?"

"I am in love with him," said Marjorie. "His church forbids him to marry so it shall be a marriage of true minds."

"She needs a good purge." (Mrs. Bassett.)

"Touch of the birch rod more like." (Mrs. Jenkins.)

"Darling child, I *feel* for you!" (Lady Beth-ons).

"Bread and water and locked in her room." (Mrs. Fyfe-Bartholomew.)

"Go to your room," said Marjorie's grand-mother severely. "I shall talk to you later."

Marjorie floated out, the stocky figure of Mackintosh ploughing after her.

Once inside her bedroom, she leaned against the door, feeling the beating of her heart against her stays. Surely it would work! Not that Father Benjamin wasn't extremely hand-some. Marjorie played briefly with a rosy fantasy of being immured in a convent and seeing him every ten years through a black, forbidding grill and then rushed to that now well-worn magazine photograph for courage.

The light began to fail outside and one by one the elderly ladies' carriages arrived to take them home. Lady Bethons was the last to leave. As Marjorie was turning up the gaslight, she heard her grandmother's slow footsteps on the stairs.

Mrs. Wilton entered and seated herself on a small chair beside the popping and hissing gas fire.

"Now, Marjorie," she began, arranging her skirts, "you are a very silly girl. I will say no more about it provided I have your promise to forget this . . . this . . . priest."

"I cannot," said Marjorie in a trembling

voice for she hated to lie to her grandmother so much. "I love him."

"Then you will stay in your room until you come to your senses!"

Marjorie picked up her rosary by way of reply and began to tell her beads.

"Ooooh! I could *shake* you," said Mrs. Wilton, rising to her feet and trembling with outrage. "I am going right round to St. Mary's to give that young man a piece of my mind."

Marjorie experienced a terrible qualm of conscience. She had been forward enough in approaching Father Benjamin herself, welcoming him to the suburb. Their conversations had been innocent in the extreme.

But she must have that Season in London. She could only hope that Father Benjamin would refuse to see Mrs. Wilton.

Finding that she was getting no reaction whatsoever, Mrs. Wilton stumped angrily out. She was becoming seriously worried. There was only one answer to the problem of Marjorie. The girl must be married off as soon as possible.

She rang for her carriage and told the surprised coachman to take her to St. Mary's.

Father Benjamin was extremely puzzled as to why this elderly lady should be calling on him. Mrs. Wilton merely said calmly that she believed Father Benjamin had made himself known to her granddaughter and then sat back and fixed the young priest with a steely glare. Had Father Benjamin been less innocent he would have immediately understood Mrs. Wilton's problem and have allayed her fears.

But his childlike blue eyes merely lit up with enthusiasm and he said in a pleasant Irish brogue, "Ah, that's a fine girl you have there, Mrs. Wilton. You are Anglican I believe. A pity. We could do with some fine-looking lasses like Miss Montmorency-James to liven up our little flock."

"There will be no livening up of your little flock," snapped Mrs. Wilton.

Father Benjamin merely smiled. He was already used to several irascible old ladies in his own congregation. He assumed Mrs. Wilton was trying to be funny in a grumpy way. He also assumed she had only called to be neighborly, having freshly come from Ireland and not quite realized the immense barriers between the Anglican and Catholic religions.

"Sure, it was neighborly of you to call, Mrs. Wilton," he said in a jolly voice. "I look forward to the pleasure of seeing your beautiful daughter on my walks."

"May I point out you have not been introduced to her," said Mrs. Wilton.

"Oh, but I have," said Father Benjamin. "The young lady introduced herself in a most friendly way."

"Let me put things another way," sighed Mrs. Wilton. "You are a man of God and cannot become married."

A look of rather pleasant stupidity crossed Father Benjamin's blue eyes. "No," he said. "That's a fact for sure, for sure. Would you be wanting a cup of tea?"

"No, I would not," rapped out Mrs. Wilton. "I will come directly to the point. You will not be seeing my granddaughter again."

"Ah, well, now. She'll be making her coming out and all that," said Father Benjamin with infuriating good humor. "And next time I see her, she'll be married to a lord, I shouldn't wonder. Will you be taking a house up in town?"

Mrs. Wilton stared at him in baffled fury. Then slowly the anger died out of her eyes. Plainly this cunning priest was determined not to understand. But a Season for Marjorie? Well, why not! "I have money enough," thought Mrs. Wilton, "and society is not what it was. Money talks. Look at Jimmy Simons."

She smiled frostily at Father Benjamin. "As a matter of fact Marjorie will be leaving— next week."

She rose to her feet to conclude this useless interview.

"Don't wear yourself out at all the parties, ma'am," said Father Benjamin with a cheery grin. "And may the Lord bless you."

"What! Oh, yes, quite," said Mrs. Wilton faintly, her mind already busy with plans.

* * *

It took more than a week to effect the change. But Marjorie's rosary and crucifix and religious painting had mysteriously disappeared. The house on Haddon Common seemed to be in a perpetual uproar and servants packed and sorted and chattered with excitement over the move into high society.

Mrs. Wilton had hired a house in Belgravia and had rummaged through old diaries and address books until she had managed to find one illustrious name among her old acquaintances, that of Penelope, Lady Bywater. She had met Lady Bywater many years ago at a hotel in Deauville and the two had become very friendly. Mrs. Wilton had not, however, seen fit to resume the friendship on her native soil, feeling that one could step out of one's place abroad but in Britain, of course, the good Lord had ordained things otherwise.

Surprisingly enough, Lady Bywater was still alive and delighted to offer her help in launching young Marjorie.

Lady Bywater was to live with them in the Belgravia house until the end of the Season.

Marjorie lived in a whirl of silks and satins and lace. She was taken to that terrifying temple of *haute couture*, the House of Frederic in Lower Grosvenor Street, to be measured and pinned and fitted.

It was, in a way, rather like getting ready for a very expensive theatrical production. The house in Eaton Terrace, Belgravia, was the stage setting. The backers were consulted—in this case the backers being the modistes and jewelers and catering firms—and the costumes designed and made ready.

To Marjorie, used only to the stagnant life of Haddon Common, it was breathless and frightening. She was, after all, to play the part of the leading lady. It seemed impossible that everything should be ready in time for the "curtain up."

But one fine morning, she woke up in Eaton Terrace and found herself "on stage." Waiting in the wings was the mysterious Lady Bywater whom Marjorie had not as yet met.

She was to meet her that very day and had conjured up a picture of a sort of stage Duchess.

At first sight, Lady Bywater was a startling disappointment. She was, first of all, very old. She was as thin and tall as Mrs. Wilton was small and fat. She wore a shaggy white wig decorated with artificial flowers and was dressed in a long trailing black velvet gown that smelled unpleasantly of sweat and mothballs. Around her scrawny neck, she wore an *enclavage*, that type of necklace that goes round and round the neck several times and then falls to the navel in a cascade of jewels. The jewels were so large and gaudy that Marjorie could hardly believe they were real.

She had pale myopic eyes and tobacco-stained false china teeth that made irritating clicking sounds. Marjorie felt fashionably doomed from the start but Mrs. Wilton seemed to find nothing amiss with her aristocratic guest and treated Lady Bywater with uncharacteristic deference.

"So this is the gel," said Lady Bywater, raising a lorgnette that was held together with ginger-beer wire and staring at Marjorie from head to foot. "She'll do, Mary, she'll *take*. I've got us invitations to old Crummers's ball tonight. That's a good place to launch her."

"Who on earth is old Crummers?" thought Marjorie drearily envisioning a Season of partying and dancing with every septuagenarian in London.

"Crummers?" she queried politely without much hope.

"The Duchess of Dunster, my dear," explained Lady Bywater not knowing that with these magic words she had transferred herself into Marjorie's fairy godmother. "She's a lot younger than me but we used to be friendly. I always used to call her Crummers though I forget why."

Marjorie suddenly felt terrified. It was all too soon. The Duchess of Dunster was Lord Philip's mother. She would see him that very evening!

All of a sudden her fantasy about marrying Lord Philip seemed ridiculous. In the quiet of Haddon Common, there had been nothing else to do *but* dream and all dreams had seemed possible since reality was kept so far at bay. How could she have fallen in love with a *photograph*, of all things? But in the photograph, he looked like the aristocrat of her dreams—haughty and proud. It was one thing to dream about meeting a haughty young man and another to actually envisage doing it, now that that very moment had come so close. He was probably bad-tempered. He would probably glare through the silk and lace of Marjorie's expensive ball gown straight into the depths of her middle-class soul. Marjorie cautiously raised her arm and sniffed it. Perhaps one actually did smell of the shop after all and she had been, all unaware, exuding an aroma of sugar and spices and blacking and tallow candles.

She began to suffer from acute stage fright. What did she know of the aristocracy apart from Lady Bywater? In Haddon Common, Lady Bywater would be considered an eccentric frump. But she seemed strangely to belong to this new milieu of Belgravia. And just look at this house!

By the rich living standards of the wealthy middle class, it did not seem to amount to much. Mrs. Wilton had rented it furnished. It was Marjorie's first inkling of the strange parsimony of the aristocracy. Nothing in the furnishings that could still conceivably be used had been thrown away. Faded Chinese wallpaper lined the walls. Spindly furniture dating from the Regency was sparsely set about the room. The curtains at the windows were of the finest silk but sadly threadbare in patches. The rugs were Oriental but very well worn and almost bare in places. There was no gaslight in the bedrooms and one had to take a candle up to bed. A set of Hogarth prints in black wood frames ornamented the staircase, depicting gin-sodden women nursing dirty babies and horrible little boys disemboweling cats or hanging dogs from the lamppost.

But there were certain expenses, it seemed, that were *de rigeur.* "A brace of footmen, I think," Lady Bywater was saying in her light, drawling voice. "Come just as cheap by the pair. Duties? Well, they help you out of your carriage and knock at the door when you're making calls. They serve the luncheon and clean the gold and silver and wash your small change so you don't get an infection from the tradesmen's dirty money. Iron your newspapers, brush the mud from the hems of your dresses, all that stuff. You'll need a carriage, nothing grand. A groom and a gig will do nicely and Marjorie must be taught how to handle the reins. You can use my servants and landau for more formal occasions but I expect you to pay their wages and forage. Then there's a butler. Have mine for the season. He's quite old but very imposing when he's not drunk."

Marjorie was to learn that the venerable butler was never drunk but Lady Bywater, like most of her class, put all her servants' frailties down to drink. When exhausted footmen tumbled asleep off the carriage backstrap, they were drunk.

When aged and infirm butlers stumbled on their way to answer late night calls, they had been at the master's brandy again. When a harassed housemaid broke the china, she was damned as an inebriate.

But at the moment, all Marjorie could do was shrink inside as she hovered in the wings of this new and strange world.

"Marjorie may use my lady's maid," Lady Bywater was saying. "You will pay her for her services, of course. In return for all this, I will make sure that Marjorie is introduced to the right sort of chap."

Mrs. Wilton raised a plump hand in protest. "I do not want Marjorie to move in very high circles, Lady Bywater."

"Why ever not?" Lady Bywater stared curiously at the plump figure of her friend. "What on earth is the point of all this expense?"

Mrs. Wilton's face became suffused with a delicate pink. "I think it would be better if Marjorie could fix her interest with one of her

own kind . . . a doctor or a lawyer or a
Lloyd's underwriter or . . ."

"How frightfully *dull!*"

"It does not do to move out of one's class,"
said Mrs. Wilton firmly.

Lady Bywater looked quite huffy. "But you
have already done just that," she pointed out.
"You will certainly find plenty of rich middle-
class young men ornamenting the London
Season but they are not, mark you, chaperoned by *me* and I move in the first circles."

The old lady was becoming quite flustered
and Mrs. Wilton hastened to reassure her. "I
am well aware of that fact. Let us say this
Season is not entirely a means to secure
Marjorie a husband. I would simply like her
to enjoy herself and become used to the society of young men. We have no young men in
Haddon Common."

"You have no nothing in Haddon Common,"
snapped Lady Bywater, made ungrammati-
cal by irritation. "You are very rich, Mary,
and that is all that counts these days. Why,
the flower of our aristocracy have been
marrying quite impossible creatures from
America for the past decade and longer."

"Americans do not count. They are foreign-
ers," said Mrs. Wilton, sure of her ground at
last.

"It's no use talking like this," said Lady
Bywater impatiently. "I will go and organize
the servants for you. My lady's maid, Stavely,

will be here in good time to prepare Marjorie for the ball. Now, Marjorie," she went on, fixing that young lady with a steely glare, "your voice is pleasant and clear but it requires slightly more of a drawl."

"Do you wish me to speak like this, for example," said Marjorie with an uncanny imitation of Lady Bywater's upper-class drawl.

"Splendid!" said Lady Bywater. "Good-bye, my dear. Until this evening!"

"Until this evening . . . ," echoed Marjorie faintly. Oh, that it would never come.

But like Christmas and dentists' appointments, it came all too quickly. One minute the hours of freedom seemed to stretch out in front of Marjorie, and the next minute it seemed she was standing, trembling, on the doorstep as the carriage was brought round.

In her usual way, Mrs. Wilton had told Marjorie she looked "very well." Privately, Mrs. Wilton was alarmed. Marjorie had blossomed in one evening under the expert hands of a lady's maid into a young lady of quite startling beauty.

The new sueded tricot corset with lace trimming that Marjorie wore under her evening ensemble had thrust her bosom forward one way and her posterior the other, giving her girlish figure an air of voluptuous maturity. She was wearing a white lace evening bodice with pagoda sleeves, which was securely hooked onto a heavy silk "mermaid" skirt—so called because it fitted tightly over the hips and then flared out from the knees in a fishtail effect. Her soft brown hair was dressed low on her forehead and threaded with white jasmine flowers made of delicate silk. A heavy choker of real pearls secured by a diamond clasp—rented—supported her slender neck.

Her white silk evening shoes had long pointed toes and Louis heels. Over the whole, she wore a white velvet cloak, three-quarter length, and gathered at the hem at the back. Its high collar and hem were ornamented with rich silver embroidery.

Mrs. Wilton was resplendent in lilac crêpe and Lady Bywater wore her favorite black velvet.

The ladies were assisted into Lady Bywater's landau by the "brace" of footmen, hired that very day from an agency.

The Dunster town house was situated on Park Lane, a short drive away—too short, thought Marjorie, who felt life rushing in on her at a tremendous rate.

The landau swayed sedately through the evening streets. The weather was mild, and somewhere among the city smells of horse and smoke crept the elusive scents of late spring. Marjorie sat in the carriage in an agony of anticipation. She did not want to go to this ball. She did not want to meet Lord Philip. She wanted to creep back to Haddon

Common and play with Mackintosh and never, ever leave it again.

All too soon the carriage came to a halt. There were two majestic policemen on duty outside, resting their shiny regulation boots on a strip of red carpet.

The tantalizing, jaunty strains of a polka drifted out into the evening air. Marjorie hesitated, waiting for her cue.

"Come along, girl!" said Lady Bywater testily. "Or are you going to stand out in the street all night?"

As if walking in a dream, Marjorie moved forward toward the lighted doorway and placed one white silk-shod foot over the threshold.

She was on stage. She was In Society. There was no going back.

At first glance, the ballroom looked as if a piece of the African rain forest had found its way to Mayfair. "I think you overdid it this time, mama," remarked Lord Philip, looking down at his mother who lurked in the shade of an enormous potted fern.

"It wasn't my idea," said the Duchess of Dunster sulkily. "It was Madge Barrington's latest protégé, Cyril Wilks. He designs parties and things. 'I must have trees, trees, trees!' he kept yapping, just like a terrier. So now I have trees, trees, trees. Half of Kew Gardens, by the look of it. But everyone has Cyril you know. It's frightfully up-to-date."

"Aren't you frightened your guests might get lost in the undergrowth or start sporting with Amaryllis in the shade?"

The Duchess was not of a literary turn of mind. "Sport with who? . . . oh, never mind. Their morals are their own concern. There's room enough to dance. It just gets a bit overgrown around the perimeter. By the way, you have to ask a Miss Montmorency-James for a dance."

"Never heard of her."

"Nobody has. The Montmorency bit is from the mother whose family were wealthy haberdashers. The James bit is the father who owned grocery stores. Both dead. The grandmother is a Mrs. Wilton and she *is* Wilton's groceries, Wilton's tea, Wilton's butter and I don't know what else. The girl is rich."

"I'm not looking for an heiress," said Lord Philip. "You really must stop trying to arrange marriages for me."

"I'm not," said the Duchess crossly. "The girl is being chaperoned by Riddles, you know, Penelope Bywater. All you need to do is give her a dance and introduce her to some chaps from the City. Grandmother wants her to marry middle-class money. Here they come. Hello, Riddles!"

"Evening, Crummers," drawled Lady Bywater. She presented Marjorie and Mrs. Wilton.

Marjorie kept her eyes firmly glued to the

floor. One glance at Lord Philip had been enough to confirm her worst fears. He was arrogant and frightening and did not look in the least pleased to see her.

In that, she was wrong. Lord Philip had been taken aback by her very feminine beauty and in normal circumstances would have set himself to please but at that moment, a very attractive debutante, Amy Featherington, came up with her parents to shake his hand and Lord Philip, after asking Marjorie for a waltz and signing his name hurriedly in her dance card, promptly forgot about her and turned his not inconsiderable charm on Amy.

And Marjorie, watching the play of that famous charm from a little way away, fell headlong in love with Lord Philip all over again. She studied Amy to try to find out the attraction this girl had for Lord Philip.

She was a very frilly, feminine miss with wide blue eyes and light brown hair that had a strange smell of burnt feathers. Amy had just spent twelve hours having one of the new permanents inflicted on her head but Marjorie did not as yet know that. She had a lisping little voice. "Does oo want to dance wif ickle me?" she said, looking up at Philip from under her long eyelashes while Marjorie studied every word and gesture.

Marjorie glanced back at Lord Philip. He really was a remarkably handsome man. His face was slightly tanned and his eyes were of a brilliant, intense blue with long curling black lashes. He had a firm chin and a humorous, sensuous mouth. His hair was not black as she had guessed from the photograph but dark brown streaked with gold. His evening coat was molded to his broad shoulders and the collar of his shirt was at least eight centimeters high. When he was not trying to charm, however, his face resumed the stern and arrogant expression of the photograph.

Then Marjorie no longer had any time to study him. Her dance card was quickly filled, Lady Bywater having put it around London society that she was a wealthy heiress. A lot of the aristocracy were feeling the pinch and did not care where the money came from as long as it came.

Marjorie hardly noticed her partners and answered their conversational sallies mechanically. She was intent on watching Lord Philip.

Lord Philip found he was looking forward to his waltz with Miss Marjorie. Amy's simpering baby talk had grated on his nerves and he no longer found her appealing. Marjorie was an exquisite dancer and he had been very much aware of her.

Marjorie noticed the look of increasing boredom on his face and wondered what to do. She had rapidly been rehearsing the role of Amy. Now that would not do and she did not have time to find another. The fact that Lord Philip might like her for herself never once crossed Marjorie's agonized mind.

And so it was that Lord Philip found the reality so much less enjoyable than the anticipation and a strangely silent Marjorie, when it came her turn to dance with him, moved stiffly and awkwardly in his arms and said not a word.

He experienced a pang of disappointment. He had thought Marjorie might prove to be something out of the ordinary.

"Are you enjoying the ball?" he asked politely, while his bored, restless eyes ranged over the floor.

"Yes," whispered Marjorie, staring into his chest. At last Marjorie found the courage to raise her eyes only to find he was no longer paying any attention to her. She wondered what she was doing wrong. She worried and wondered about it so much that she could barely enjoy the pleasure of being held in his arms and it seemed no time at all before the precious dance was over. She watched him in wide-eyed dismay over the shoulder of her next partner. Lord Philip seemed to be much taken with his new partner, a thin, angular girl in a long beaded gown.

"I shall study *her*," thought poor Marjorie.

Her large eyes noticed that Lord Philip had left the floor with his partner and disappeared into the shrubbery. A pang of pure jealousy stabbed through Marjorie's bosom. No sooner had her present dance ended than she scanned her dance card. The next two dances were taken up by a fictitious Mr. Hubert. Marjorie had written his name several times in her card hoping to keep two or three spaces free for Lord Philip.

She gently glided toward the banked jungle of ferns into which Lord Philip had disappeared with his partner.

A pair of eyes, sharpened by jealousy, watched her go. Hermoine Ffofington considered herself more or less unofficially engaged to Lord Philip. Both were of a cynical turn of mind. They had been childhood friends. Somehow there had always seemed to be an unspoken agreement between them that they would eventually settle down together after they had had their fun. Hermione had calmly watched one impressionable debutante after another falling head over heels in love with Philip and had also enjoyed their eventual and inevitable dismay when he quickly lost interest.

But this Marjorie-girl disturbed her. Marjorie was beautiful in a strange and disturbing way. She quietly followed Marjorie into the shrubbery.

Unaware that he had two hidden listeners, Lord Philip was suffering the outpourings of his partner. She had seemed like such a good sort on the few occasions when he had spoken

to her before. Now she seemed most absolutely and frightfully nuts. Her name was
Jessie Wuthers. She had begged a word with
him in private in an intense sort of way that
had led Lord Philip to hope for the best. But
it seemed that all she wanted to do was talk
about Art and Life and Shared Thoughts. She
had very black hair and an intense white face
and high Slavic cheekbones. Her speech was
abrupt and clipped. Philip realized to his
acute embarrassment that his few light flir-
tatious remarks had been taken as signs of
intense fellow feeling.

"You are too much a gentleman to say so,"
Jessie said, staring up at him with eyes like
two pieces of jet, "but I have this, you know,
jolly sort of feeling of Being at Home with
Somebody."

"Quite," said Lord Philip, easing a finger
into his high collar.

"How *fast!*" thought Marjorie in amazement
from behind the shadow of a giant fern. She
could not hear Lord Philip's reply.

"I mean," Jessie was pressing on, "all this
rot about the conventions is ridiculous."

"She is going to say something about two
hearts beating as one," thought Lord Philip
in desperation.

She did.

"But when Two Hearts Beat as One," said
Jessie with an awkward laugh, "intelligent

people like us can throw convention to the winds. Have you read Elinor Glyn?"

"No, I haven't," said Philip crossly. "Look, it's frightfully hot and all that. Let me get you some refreshment."

Marjorie parted the fronds of the fern and peered through. Lord Philip had taken Jessie's arm in a firm grasp that looked downright loverlike to Marjorie's jealous eyes and was leading her out of the interior decorator's jungle.

"That must be what he admires!" thought Marjorie in amazement. She immediately began to practice her new role, unaware that she too was being spied on.

Hermione watched curiously as Marjorie's face somehow took on the sharp overeager features of Jessie Wuthers. Her eyes sparkled with malice. Philip simply must learn of this.

Her next dance was with Lord Philip and fortunately it was the inevitable waltz, which gave ample opportunity for conversation.

Lord Philip looked down at Hermione Ffofington's face with pleasure. Good old Hermione! Always the same. He knew he would marry her one day and sometimes he felt it should be quite soon.

He was not getting any younger and at thirty-two felt he was fast approaching middle age. Lord Philip was very old-fashioned in his ideas of marriage. He did not exactly believe in a marriage of true minds, he certainly did not believe in love, but he did believe in marrying a girl of one's class who would bring some valuable agricultural property into the marriage. He had all the canniness and instinct for survival of the true aristocrat. He also had the aristocrat's rather rigid mind, which was at most times well disguised by his good looks and famous charm. He enjoyed flirting with marriageable girls and occasionally having affairs with unmarriageable ones. He did not consider himself a snob and was capable of enjoying the company of someone from the lower ranks like, say, a Marjorie Montmorency-James. He expected them, however, to know their place and so far, those inhabitants of the lesser classes that he had to date favored with his notice had done just that.

Hermione would make a good wife, he thought. She was as smart as paint this evening in her cleverly cut pink silk gown. Her dark brown hair was becomingly dressed and her patrician nose gave her face an air of authority. She had rather small, twinkling, intelligent eyes and a tongue like a razor. He enjoyed her company very much.

"What do you think of the grocer's girl?" she was asking.

"Oh, Miss Montmorency-James? Very disappointing. I had expected her to have more character."

"Ask her for another dance," commanded Hermione, grinning up at him wickedly. "You'll find she has mysteriously become Jessie Wuthers."

"What are you talking about?"

"The clever Marjorie thinks you are smitten with Jessie and so she has been studying the role of Jessie. She's very good. I saw her rehearsing in the shrubbery and she really should be on the stage!"

"I say!" said Lord Philip. "What a joke!" He looked across the ballroom floor to where Marjorie was expertly swaying in the arms of a thin young man. She looked very fresh, very virginal, very beautiful.

"No, you must be mistaken," he said, looking back at Hermione. "She is not cunning enough. She looks a complete innocent to me."

"Oh, she is," said Hermione, "an innocent who is very much in love."

"Love!" Philip's mobile mouth curled in distaste and Hermione kept a fixed bright smile on her face. She was deeply in love with Philip herself but she knew his views on the subject and kept her emotions well hidden.

"Oh, don't look so stern," Hermione teased. "Do give the little chameleon a dance. I wonder what would happen if she fell in love with two fellows at once. Probably split herself in two."

"I shall do nothing of the kind," he said. "I obliged her with one dance to please mama—

the girl's sponsor is one of her old friends—
but it does not do to pay girls of that class too
much attention. It can lead to all sorts of
embarrassment. She'll soon be happily married
to a stockbroker or some such chap. Goodness
knows, there have been enough of my own
kind in love with me for my title and my
fortune. Everybody loves a lord, you see. Except you, dear Hermione. We are two of a
kind."

"You sound just like Jessie Wuthers,"
mocked Hermione. "She always says things
like that. But do dance with Marjorie, Philip.
You can be such a stuffed shirt at times."

"Oh, very well. But I shall prove you wrong.
You are coming on my little picnic tomorrow?"

"I'll think about it," teased Hermione although her heart cried out that the stars
would reel in their courses before she would
give up an opportunity of spending some time
with Philip.

Philip was very annoyed to find that he
had allowed himself to engage Miss Montmorency-James for the supper dance. Marjorie
had scribbled the mysterious Mr. Hubert's
name in that space in the wild hope that he
would ask her.

The dance proved to be a rowdy set of the
Lancers and he had no opportunity for conversation with her. She seemed a lively, pretty, animated girl and he thought Hermione
must have been imagining things.

But no sooner were they seated at a little table in the supper room than the fun began. The ferns and palm trees seemed to have grown over into the supper room and the dining couples were mostly hidden from each other. He was bitterly glad that there was no one else around to witness this silly girl's odd behavior.

He raised his eyes from the plump quail on his plate to find himself looking at Jessie Wuthers.

Only it wasn't Jessie of course, but it was a miracle how Marjorie strangely seemed to *become* Jessie. Her large expressive eyes seemed to turn small and sharp and she hunched her shoulders in a way that turned her pretty figure into a parody of Jessie's lean, angular one.

"Don't you find the conventions of society so restricting?" breathed Marjorie-Jessie intensely.

"No, I like them," he replied in a repressive voice.

"Ah, you tease and joke," cried Marjorie with a mad laugh. "But when Two Hearts Beat in Unison, what are conventions?"

"A bloody good way of stopping people from having illegitimate babies," he said nastily.

His use of that awful and shocking swear word should have given Marjorie pause but instead she thought he was responding boldly to the Marjorie-Jessie-throw-away-the-conventions image.

She threw back her head and pealed out a fair imitation of Jessie's shrill laugh.

"Don't do that!" he said involuntarily.

"Don't what?" said Marjorie, round-eyed.

"Act like Jessie Wuthers," he said patiently. "The woman with the black hair with whom I was dancing. The one in the beaded dress. She's a good sort and I shouldn't be discussing her but she does talk the most awful twaddle and one of her is quite enough."

Marjorie turned crimson with humiliation. Now that she no longer had a role to hide behind, she felt very young and silly and inexperienced. She was acutely aware that she was *tête-à-tête* with a Duke's son, that she herself was middle class, that marriage to him had been a silly daydream, that she had been discovered behaving like a fool. And she wished she were dead.

Marjorie's wide dark eyes looked up into Lord Philip's blue ones and then fell miserably to her plate, her thick black lashes fanning out against her cheek.

Lord Philip caught some of Marjorie's humiliation, which had been reflected in that one glance, and was uncomfortably reminded of a dream he had had where he had walked into the Atheneum to take tea with a bishop and had found on entering the club that he was not wearing any trousers. He tried to change the conversation.

"I believe my mother's old friend, Lady Bywater, is staying with you?"

"Yes."

"And this is your first ball of the Season?"

"Yes."

Lord Philip sighed. The girl would not look up. She would not eat. He had done enough and if she wanted to sit there and be miserable, then he was happy to leave her to it. He tried to concentrate on his food and drank quite a lot of Château Lafitte very quickly.

A jaunty tune drifted in from the ballroom— "Champagne Charlie is my name . . ."—as the dance recommenced. The air was warm and heavy with perfume and French chalk and pomade and there was an almost tangible undercurrent of heavy sensuality. Oh, we obeyed the conventions all right. We did not touch in public. But we were aware of the excitement of forbidden liaisons and the stealthy creep along the corridor of some country house in the small hours of the morning; the stuffy, smelly intimacy of the hansom cab whose heavily bribed driver promenaded his tired horse round and round the park until the dawn came up. Intrigue was what made the social world go round, not love. But there was always the memory of that first dance, that first Season. Out of this jumble of thoughts, Lord Philip abruptly re-

membered his own. He remembered how lost
and awkward he had felt and how sophisti-
cated and *old* the girls of his own age had
appeared. How hard and calculating the eyes
of their mamas. He felt an unaccustomed
twinge of compassion for the crumpled young
thing opposite.

He tried again.

"You are living in Eaton Terrace, I believe."

"Yes," whispered a little voice from the
other side of the table.

"Where is your home normally. I mean
when you're not in London for the Season?"

"Haddon Common."

"Where's that? Outside London?" He was
suddenly determined to wring a whole sentence out of her.

"Norwood. Near Norwood."

"And what's it like?"

"Very pleasant, thank you."

"It must be something more descriptive
than 'very pleasant.' What is the social life
like?"

"Oh," faltered Marjorie. "Not much. I go for
walks on the common with my dog, Mackintosh. My grandmother entertains her friends,
of course, but they are all very old. And I go
to church and . . . and . . . we have a weekly
sewing bee . . . and . . . and . . ."

"Sounds absolutely frightful. I should die
of boredom."

Marjorie's eyes flew up and she said in a

stronger voice, "Well, it does seem dull I suppose but it . . . it's *safe*, you know, and everyone is so kind . . ."

"Most of us here are quite kind," remarked Philip, relieved to see she had picked up her knife and fork and was attempting to eat. "Have some wine. It's very good and it will buck you up no end."

Marjorie had never drunk anything stronger than cider but she dutifully took a cautious sip from her glass. It tasted like medicine. So she drank it like medicine, tipping the glass and swallowing the contents in one gulp.

She began to feel a little glow starting in the pit of her stomach and spreading through the rest of her body. He poured her another glass and she swallowed some of it cautiously. It really wasn't bad once you became used to it, reflected Marjorie, mentally damning a very good vintage with faint praise.

The gray world of her misery began to recede, began to take on color.

"Do you have many social engagements?" asked Lord Philip, noticing for the first time what remarkable eyes the girl had. They changed like the sea, one minute dark, dark gray and the next almost light silver.

"I don't know," said Marjorie shyly. "Lady Bywater is arranging everything."

"Does she plan to marry you off?"

"I don't think so," said Marjorie. "My grandmother wants me to become used to the society of young people. There are no young people in Haddon Common, you see."

"Come, all young ladies wish to get married," teased Philip, admiring the tiny gold flecks in her brown hair. He bestowed a smile of singular sweetness on her and Marjorie's heart began to hammer against her stays. "You'll find plenty of suitable chaps," he went on. "I have some jolly stockbroker friends you would like very much."

Philip had no intention of being or sounding snobbish but his light remark about stockbroker friends put Marjorie firmly in her middle-class place. She drank her wine very quickly, looking for that magic glow. She said:

"Do you think I should marry a stockbroker because they are an estimable breed of young men or because I am from the middle class and can only marry someone middle class?"

"I didn't say that," snapped Philip, aware for the first time that that is exactly what he had meant. But she had made him feel badly behaved, a new and uncomfortable feeling that he wished to dispel as quickly as possible. "Look here," he said, "I'm making up a picnic party. We're going to drive down to a little place on the river tomorrow. Would you care to join us? I will ask your grandmother's permission if you like."

"Oh, *thank* you!" said Marjorie with stars in her eyes.

Something prompted him to go on, "Yes, you'll like my friends, I think, especially Hermione Ffofington. She is a great friend of mine."

"Thank you," said Marjorie again but in a more subdued voice.

He found himself becoming fascinated by those expressive eyes. Her skin was quite beautiful as well, very white and fine, and when she blushed it became suffused with a warm pink. He was acutely aware of the fact that their barrier of greenery effectively cut them off from the rest of the company. He was glad he had invited her to his picnic. He had really been too stuffy, he thought. Society had changed. King Edward himself adored the company of the rich middle class, laughed uproariously at Jewish humor and threw open the doors of his court to American heiresses. Hermione, of course, deplored the change and was always warning him against possible low-class social climbers.

He wondered for the first time whether he let Hermione influence his views too much.

He found himself wondering what his formidable brother, the Marquess of Herterford, would make of Miss Marjorie. Robert was convalescing in Deauville and had not accepted an invitation to the ball. Philip suddenly realized that brother Robert for all his stern and autocratic manner would probably like Marjorie very much. But then Robert never bothered himself with the niceties of class distinction. Which was rather a pity, thought Philip. A Marquess should be more careful in the company he kept.

Marjorie could not begin to guess at the thoughts racing behind the impassive handsome face opposite. She felt she was experiencing too much life in one chunk. She all at once wanted to leave his company and retreat back to her dreams. And if she stayed with him too long, perhaps he might regret having asked her, might even withdraw his invitation!

"It is kind of you to entertain me so well," said Marjorie shyly. "But I feel I should return to the ballroom. My next partner will be searching for me."

Lord Philip experienced a twinge of annoyance. He was not used to young ladies putting an end to any chance of holding him in conversation.

Nonetheless he got to his feet and walked round the table and drew her chair back for her. She turned and looked up at him, a drowned expression in her eyes. Marjorie was beginning to feel the effects of the wine she had drunk. She swayed slightly and he caught her arm to support her and pulled her against his chest.

Marjorie wondered whether he could hear the hammering of her heart. She stared helplessly up into his face as he bent his head slowly toward hers. She saw his firm sensuous mouth drawing closer and nearer, ever nearer . . .

"Well, what have we here!" Hermione stood staring at them, her sharp eyes sparkling with good humor while inside her feelings heaved and churned on a frothing green sea of jealousy.

"I think I drank too much wine," said Marjorie, who had jumped away from Lord Philip at the sound of Hermione's voice. "I lost my footing."

"Really, one would think you were climbing the Alps, dear girl," laughed Hermione, tapping Philip playfully on the arm with her fan. "Have you forgotten our dance, Philip? *Most* unlike you!"

"How could I ever forget *you*, Hermione," he said smiling down into her eyes in such a way that the storm inside Hermione died away and broke out a few feet away in the chaste bosom of Miss Montmorency-James. He held out an arm to each young lady and led them back into the warmth and noise of the ballroom where the faces were more flushed and glistening and the dancing more bouncing and lively.

Marjorie was quickly claimed by her partner, a young Mr. Jeffrey Lewis, son of a merchant banker and considered quite a catch despite his cheerful rugger-bugger features and his ability to treat any ballroom like a rugby scrum. As Mr. Lewis cheerfully bounced her off into the throng, plying her hand vigorously like a pump handle, she caught a fleeting glimpse of Hermione in Lord Philip's arms. He was laughing at something she was saying and looked well content. "I wasted my time with Amy and Jessie," thought Marjorie dismally. "Hermione is my rival. But there is hope. Surely there is hope."

On and on went the dance, ball gowns rustling and swishing over the floor. Round and round circled Marjorie in the arms of various young men. But she did not dance with Lord Philip again that evening. She wondered if she would ever dance with him again. Her feet ached, her head ached and she wanted to go home. But her two chaperones, Mrs. Wilton and Lady Bywater, were chattering in a rejuvenated way and seemed all set to last out a fortnight at least.

But at last the ball was over, at last the dance was done, and many the hearts that were broken, and Marjorie did wish they would stop playing that silly heartbreaking song over and over again.

A pale, gray dawn was frowning on London as the landau sailed home over the cobbles, swaying on its springs.

Marjorie wearily scanned the sky with the

anxious eyes of a mariner. One could not go on a picnic should the day remain as damp and chilly as this.

As if reading her thoughts, Lady Bywater said, "Lord Philip Cavendish said he wanted you to join his party today, Marjorie, and I gave my permission. He's taking some young people somewhere on the river. But there will be no question of your going unless the weather changes."

Marjorie closed her eyes, feeling tired and depressed. How difficult life was! Why couldn't she fall in love with someone who would love her back? And as the sky grew brighter and the rich went home and the poor started work, Marjorie fell fast asleep.

Chapter Three

The English discuss the weather a great deal because they can never seem to get used to its mercurial changes. The morning that had begun so gray and autumnal changed into full, blazing summer by the afternoon.

Lord Philip's party consisted of eight young people, including himself, and an elderly aunt to act as chaperone. They were conveyed out of London in two open carriages, the servants necessary to their comfort having been sent on ahead. Marjorie found to her dismay that she was to share a carriage with the bouncing Mr. Lewis—whom she bitterly felt had been invited along for her benefit—Jessie Wuthers, Amy Featherington, a close friend

of Lord Philip called Toby Anstruther and
the aged aunt.

Philip was in the leading carriage with
Hermione at his side and two handsome young
men, whose names she did not yet know,
facing them. Hermione was chattering and
elated at having three men to escort her—as
well she might, thought Marjorie sourly.

Her pleasure in her own appearance was
somewhat dimmed. Marjorie was wearing the
latest thing in "pneumonia" blouses, a trans-
parent confection of pale lilac chiffon worn
over a chemisette. Her skirt of heavy *crêpe de
chine* was in a deeper shade of lilac and was
swept up at the back into an elaborate fall of
pleats and gathers and ruching. On her carefully dressed hair, she wore a neat "pancake"
hat of lilac straw, tilted forward over her eyes
to complement the fashionable S-bend of her
figure. Her long white kid gloves clung to her
arms without a crease and her little lilac kid
boots peeped out from beneath the froufrou of
her skirts. She held her lilac parasol tilted
over her face, more to hide her sad expression
than to protect her skin from the sun.

The air was warm and balmy and full of
the smell of growing things, mixing memory
and desire and breeding all sorts of uncomfortable longings in Marjorie's bosom.

Toby Anstruther seemed quietly bored with
the whole outing, the aunt and Mr. Lewis
had fallen asleep and Amy and Jessie seemed

as saddened by Philip's not being in their carriage as Marjorie was. Marjorie studied the back of Philip's neck, admiring the glint of gold in his thick hair under the shadow of his straw hat. Hermione's face was often turned toward her companion and Marjorie studied every nuance, every gesture.

Her attention was finally claimed by Mr. Lewis who had awoken much refreshed from his nap. Wasn't the lilac jolly, he said, just like your dress, Miss Montmorency-James. He had been lucky, he said, to get a day off work to go on this outing. Lord Philip had only asked him the night before at the ball. No, he didn't know Lord Philip very well so it was dashed decent of him to allow him, Jeffrey Lewis, to tag along. Jolly amusing chap, Lord Philip. Had said he, Jeffrey, and Miss Montmorency-James made a good couple. Ha! Ha!

Marjorie winced. So she *was* being partnered off with Mr. Lewis.

Marjorie decided there and then not to lose hope. She was here and Philip was here and a picnic would provide endless opportunities for romance. She murmured polite noncommittal noises in answer to Mr. Lewis's outpourings while her mind shaped one romantic picture after another. In her mind's eye she could see the white tablecloth spread on the grass while Philip lounged beside her, propping his head on his hand. His other hand would slide across the grass to take her own and then he would suggest that they take a walk along the riverbank away from the others and under the glinting, dappling sunlight, he would get down on one knee and he would say . . ."

"We're here!" called Lord Philip.

Marjorie came out of her reverie to find that the carriage was bowling along a smooth drive between manicured lawns.

It turned out that Lord Philip liked his *al fresco* entertainments to be as rigidly and formally organized as a state reception.

The picnic was to be held at the edge of the river in the grounds of a villa belonging to one of his friends who was recovering from consumption in a clinic in Switzerland.

On the smooth grass at the river's edge, tables had been set up, covered with heavy linen cloths, and the sunlight winked on silver and crystal. Liveried servants stood ready to serve them. On a temporary bandstand near the tables, the band of the Grenadier Guards was playing airs from Gilbert and Sullivan. There were even little cards at each place so that Miss Marjorie Montmorency-James should know that she was to sit next to Mr. Lewis while Lord Philip sat at another table altogether with Hermione Ffofington.

There was only one small comfort. Marjorie's table was next to Lord Philip's and so she could watch Hermione. "Not much of my idea of a picnic," whispered Mr. Lewis. "It's outside but that's about all you can say for it."

"I think it's perfectly splendid," lied Marjorie while she strained her ears to hear what Hermione was saying. From the snatches of conversation she was able to pick up, she judged that Hermione was one of those young misses who pride themselves on speaking their minds. She was in fact very cruel in some of her observations but Lord Philip laughed appreciatively at everything she said.

Had Marjorie not been so obsessed with Lord Philip she would have noticed that his two handsome friends were eying her appreciatively. But Lord Philip did and felt vaguely irritated although he did not know why. His friends, who had shared his carriage, were a Mr. Guy Randolph and Lord Harry Belmont. Both were very much lilies of the field, neither working, toiling nor spinning. Both were of impeccable birth and both impecunious, relying on friends like Lord Philip to supply parties for their entertainment and various aunts and uncles to pay their tailors' bills. Both were looking out for an heiress to marry. Not many heiresses, thought Philip with surprise, were so awfully pretty as Marjorie.

A stand of pretty aspen trees quivered by the river and cast the moving shadows of their young leaves across Marjorie's thoughtful face. What was she brooding about, he wondered and was overcome by a desire to know.

There was lemonade or champagne for the ladies and Marjorie had decided to try champagne. She did not like the taste of it at all; in fact it did not taste nearly as pretty as it looked. She idly watched the bubbles in her glass and listened to the pleasant chuckling of the river and paid not one heed to any of the conversational efforts of Mr. Lewis.

At last the picnic meal was over and the company rose from the tables. Philip excused himself from Hermione and drew Toby Anstruther a little to one side. Toby Anstruther's long, fair and foolish face reflected its owner's usual boredom.

"Look, Toby," said Philip. "Would you mind squiring Hermione for a little? I want to have a brief word in private with Miss Montmorency-James."

"Very well, laddie," said Toby with a sigh. "Your parties are always so formal, Philip. No abandoned gaiety for you. You're a relic of the last century, you really are."

Philip expertly maneuvered Marjorie away from the rest of the company, watched by at least four pairs of jealous eyes.

"Will you walk a little way with me, Miss Montmorency-James?" asked Philip.

"To the ends of the earth," thought Marjorie. Then she remembered her role as Hermione.

"You seem to be quite a heartbreaker, Lord

Philip," said Marjorie in an amused voice. He looked down at her in surprise and found the eyes turned up to his seemed to have grown smaller and shrewder. Her movements were quicker and brisker.

"You are managing to break some hearts yourself," he said lightly. "Jeffrey Lewis seems quite smitten."

"Oh, he's just like a noisy puppy," laughed Marjorie. "He reminds me of my dog, Mackintosh, when he wants to go out for a walk. Pant, pant, pant. I expect him to come bounding up to me with a leash in his mouth."

"A very unkind observation," said Philip flatly.

"And then you have dear Amy and Jessie pining after you," went on Marjorie, too immersed in her role to notice the displeasure on his face. A little breeze had sprung up and her lilac dress fluttered and whispered along the walk. "Ickle Amy is just *dying* for your company and dear, dear Jessie pines for an opportunity to tell you how two hearts can beat as one."

"Miss Montmorency-James," he said savagely. "I would like to talk to *you*. I have an awful feeling you are imitating someone and from the tone of your conversation that someone must be quite terrible . . ."

He broke off in consternation. Surely Marjorie could not be imitating Hermione? But

the tone of the voice, the eyes, the brittle
derision were all too familiar.

"I wasn't imitating anyone," said Marjorie
in a low voice. "I was just trying to be fashionable. Everyone seems to talk that way."

"Well, they shouldn't," said Philip, wondering in amazement how he had ever found
such conversation amusing.

They had been walking along a paved path
that was shaded on either side by trees. It
ended abruptly and Marjorie half turned to
go back when she gave a little exclamation.

"Look!" she cried in delight.

The sunlight filtered down through a small
wood in front of them. A hazy blue, like
smoke, curled round the boles of the trees.
Bluebells! Masses of them. Unmindful of possible damage to her skirt, Marjorie edged
forward through the trees until she found
herself in the middle of a small clearing.

"Come!" she called back to Lord Philip.
"Isn't it beautiful!"

Lord Philip stood at the edge of the clearing and stared at her. She was completely
absorbed in the scene around her, rather like
a child looking at a Christmas tree. It was
very quiet except for the muted murmur of
the river. The sun struck down into the glade
in long shafts of light and the air was heavy
with the damp, hot smell of the woods.

Marjorie stood, young and graceful, among

the bluebells, as exquisite in the pastoral setting as a figure in a Watteau painting.

Lord Philip all of a sudden wanted to kiss her although he did not stop to wonder why or what the results of such an unconventional action would be. With characteristic single-mindedness, he moved slowly toward her. And Marjorie instinctively knew what he was about to do and her heart seemed to stand very still.

"Bluebells!" screamed Hermione from the edge of the clearing and the spell was broken. Toby Anstruther followed, shrugging slightly as Philip looked at him to indicate that he had been unable to keep Hermione away.

"What fun!" Hermione was crying. "Aren't they *duveen!* Just the color of that old gown Jessie's wearing although we're not supposed to *know* it's old since she's just had it dyed and altered. So proud of it too, poor little intense thing!"

And Philip, who had thought Marjorie's imitation of Hermione an extreme caricature, now realized it had in fact been a faithful copy and found himself almost disliking his old friend and felt irrationally cross with Marjorie for having been the cause of it.

"Oh, don't pick them," wailed Marjorie as Hermione stooped to pick an armful of bluebells. "They die so quickly, you know."

"Exactly like Jessie," mocked Hermione

with a wicked look at Philip. "Now she . . . er . . . *dyes* very quickly indeed."

This sally was received with all the stony silence it deserved and Hermione gave a brittle laugh.

"I don't want the stupid things anyway," she said, throwing the bluebells to the ground and taking Philip's arm. "Come along, my devoted cavalier," she said, smiling up at him. "We are going to have a little dancing and you shall partner me."

She and Philip led the way, leaving Marjorie to follow with Toby.

Marjorie looked sorrowfully back at the glade. The crushed bluebells that Hermione had thrown down looked like a shocking piece of vandalism. Marjorie was a very normal young lady and so she began to hate Hermione with all her heart and soul. She felt obscurely disappointed in Philip. How could he possibly prefer the company of such a female instead of someone warm and loving like herself?

"I hope you don't expect me to partner you, Miss Marjorie," said Toby languidly. "I never dance."

"I don't expect anything," snapped Marjorie, glaring at the couple in front. How close their heads were together. Hermione was whispering. What was she saying?

"There's no need to be so rude," replied Toby, roused to rare animation.

"You were the one who was rude," argued

Marjorie, roused to rare spirit by misery. "It was very conceited of you to think I might be panting to dance with *you*."

"I did not think anything of the kind," said Toby. "I am not a social animal. I do not care for these affairs."

"Then why come?"

"Because life is so utterly boring that it really doesn't matter what I do."

Marjorie took a deep breath. Hermione's teasing laugh floated back to her. "Only boring people find life boring," she said in a sweet voice. "I agree it doesn't matter what you do just so long as you do not inflict your boredom on anyone else."

"I say," gasped Toby, who felt as if she had just poured a bucket of cold water over him. "One does not talk like that in society, Miss Marjorie. One is polite at all times."

"Oh, *really*," said Marjorie nastily. "I hadn't noticed to date but then I have had such bad models, you see."

"Wait a bit," said Toby with a sudden laugh that transformed his normally vacuous features into something approaching good looks. "This is all wrong, you know. I tell you what. We'll begin again. Let me introduce myself. My name is Toby Anstruther and you are Miss Marjorie Montmorency-James and I am delighted to make your acquaintance. Isn't the weather hot for the time of year?"

"Very hot, sir," said Marjorie, her bad temper melting. How charming he was when he smiled.

"And may I compliment you on your blouse? Very fetching."

"Thank you, kind sir," said Marjorie demurely, although noting the fact that she must remember that one said "bloose" and not "blouse."

"In fact," went on Toby in his lazy drawl, "I believe we are to have some dancing and although I do not normally dance and certainly not as a rule on someone's damp lawn, I would very much like to dance with you, Miss Marjorie."

Marjorie glanced shyly up at him from under the shade of her parasol. His face was animated by a very sweet smile.

"Please say you will," he went on. "I know that rude fellow who was talking to you a few moments ago and saying things about he never danced may have put you off. But we've got rid of that fellow now, haven't we?"

"I hope so," said Marjorie, smiling warmly at him. "And I should very much like to dance with you, Mr. Anstruther."

"Now, what is that infuriating girl up to?" thought Lord Philip angrily as Marjorie danced under the trees in the arms of Toby Anstruther. Not content with ruining his pleasure in Hermione's company with her damned childish mimicry, she now seemed hell-bent on seducing his best friend. And succeeding very well too, if that fatuous look on Toby's stupid face was anything to go by. Funny, he had never before noticed how really stupid Toby looked!

Philip was overcome by a desire to flirt with Hermione just to show . . . just to show . . . well, just to show someone something. Anyway, he, Philip, didn't really go in for all these broken-down social barriers instigated by Kingie. It was all very well for His Majesty to be so liberal, but the aristocracy remained the aristocracy by keeping their distance and not letting any encroaching little shopkeepers' daughters disturb the *status quo*.

He whirled Hermione round and round in a waltz until she was giddy and fell breathlessly against him. He held her to him for a minute, smiling warmly down into her eyes. His acting was very good, driving that consummate actress, Miss Marjorie Montmorency-James, to greater efforts. She dazzled, she charmed, she flirted, made bold by hurt and rage. Jessie and Amy glowered on the sidelines as the gentlemen with the exception of Lord Philip nearly fought with each other over which one should have the honor of partnering Marjorie for the next dance.

Philip had just told Hermione that Marjorie's latest impersonation had been of *her* and she was thirsting for revenge.

Marjorie had never enjoyed such male adulation before and began to manage to forget

Lord Philip's presence for whole minutes at a time.

The party ended to the strains of the *Merry Widow* waltz as the sun burned down over the river and a faint chill crept through the air.

The party piled into the carriages, all saying loudly and quite ferociously what a ripping time they had had.

Hermione was strangely silent. The glimmerings of an idea of how to get even with the infuriating Marjorie was dawning in her brain.

She would speak to Philip about it.

Now, Lord Philip Cavendish might not have listened to any idea of revenge but at that moment he twisted his head round to look at the carriage behind. Miss Montmorency-James, carried away by social success and champagne, was performing the part of Lord Philip Cavendish to perfection, egged on by admiring whoops from Mr. Lewis and malicious titters from Amy and Jessie. He would not have recognized himself—whoever does? —had not a treacherous breeze wafted Mr. Lewis's exuberant comment to his listening ears. "By Jove," he howled. "If that ain't Philip to the life!"

Hermione had also heard Mr. Lewis's remark and had noticed the angry, tight look on Philip's face. Her glimmering of an idea had formed into a fully fledged plan. She leaned forward toward Lord Philip and began to whisper earnestly.

Next day Marjorie was delighted to receive an invitation from Hermione to tea that very afternoon. She did not like Hermione but she felt sure Lord Philip would be there. Marjorie felt quite drunk with power. She had only to bat her eyelids and men fell at her feet! It would not be long before Lord Philip joined the queue.

The Ffofingtons lived in Eaton Square, just around the corner, and Marjorie wondered whether to drive the short distance and arrive in style, but Lady Bywater would not hear of her carriage being used for such a short journey.

So promptly at four-thirty, Marjorie set out on foot in all the glory of a blond lace tea gown, shady straw hat with large silk tea roses and primrose-yellow gloves.

She found to her surprise that she was the last to arrive—not knowing that the others had been invited a half hour before to plot her downfall.

She was aware of a rather constrained atmosphere in the drawing room, however, and an absence of male guests. Lord Philip was certainly there but there were no other men, only Amy and Jessie and a tall, flamboyant, rather stagy-looking woman who reminded Marjorie slightly of Lady Bethons.

The newcomer was introduced as Joanna Tyson, "the famous poetess." She was wearing a long, angry-looking dress that seemed to have lots of little things bristling on it. It was trimmed with prickly black feathers at the neck and ornamented with sharp little beads. It had a strange pattern of pointy fairies with sharp eyes, long sharp noses, pointed feet and very pointed nails.

Her wide black hat was ornamented by what looked like a whole pile of glittering steel *things* that all looked vaguely like some sort of weapon of defense but were not. It must have weighed a ton and perhaps that explained the discontented droop of the poetess's mouth and the black circles under her eyes.

She bowed slightly to Marjorie and then turned her whole attention to Lord Philip. And he? He seemed to be absolutely enraptured. Not one glance did he spare poor Marjorie who sank dismally into a chair.

"Have some more tea," offered Hermione, coming up to Marjorie.

"I've had nothing yet, so I can't take more," said Marjorie crossly, unconsciously echoing Alice at the Mad Hatter's tea party.

"I'll get you some, *dear*," whispered Hermione, surprising Marjorie very much by giving her hand a sympathetic squeeze.

Hermione returned with a cup of tea and drew a chair up next to Marjorie.

Hermione had, of course, urged Philip to court the poetess in order to see what Miss Montmorency-James made of *that* role.

"Isn't it too bad," whispered Hermione, while Marjorie stared dismally at Philip over the rim of her cup. "Philip *adores* anyone who can write poetry. When that wretched woman is around he just doesn't see anyone else. In fact, he is having a poetry reading at his home tomorrow—at his mother's, you know—and we'll need to listen to all that rot."

"Will they be *her* poems?" asked Marjorie curiously.

"Mostly, I suppose," said Hermione. "The only reason Philip doesn't marry Joanna is because she is simply too old. Lord help us all if some young and beautiful thing shows a talent for writing poetry! You don't write any, I suppose?"

"No-o-o," said Marjorie slowly. "I've never tried."

"Well don't," replied Hermione with a toss of her head. "Philip will just fall head over heels in love with you if you do."

"Oh!" said Marjorie blankly while she sipped her Lapsong Suchong.

The rest of the visit was agony for Marjorie. She quite warmed toward Hermione who was being so sympathetic.

"I might try," said Marjorie at last.

"Try what?" asked Hermione eagerly.

"Well," hesitated Marjorie. "I might try to

write some poetry. Oh, it's not that I'm interested in Lord Philip. It's just . . . well . . . I think I might."

"Oh, *do*," breathed Hermione. "I hate to see Joanna monopolizing Philip. I would rather it was one of *us*." And she squeezed Marjorie's hand again and Marjorie liked her more and more. It was a small comfort. Philip never once looked at her. Never once noticed the ravishing tea gown or the pretty hat, not to mention the primrose-yellow gloves. He stared into Joanna's eyes and hung on every word. "Tomorrow he will look at me like that," vowed Marjorie, and longed to get away and begin composing.

But after the tea was over, there was a ball to prepare for, then the ball to attend and Philip was not there but Mr. Lewis was and what sort of inspiration was *that?*

But at last, the indefatigable Lady Bywater allowed Marjorie to go home. She kissed her grandmother goodnight and fairly fled to her room.

She fidgeted and fumed until the maid had gone through the ritual of brushing her hair and bringing her hot milk.

At last the house was quiet and, hunched in her kimono, Marjorie crept down to the drawing room and carefully sat down at the small writing desk in the corner. She arranged several sheets of blank paper in front of her, dipped her pen into the inkwell and thought hard. She thought and thought and thought until, at last, as the sky began to grow lighter outside and the birds began to chirp from the rooftops, she began to write.

So anxious was Marjorie about the poetry reading that she arrived at the Duchess of Dunster's a full hour before the event was to take place.

The butler informed her that Lord Philip had stepped out for a few minutes and that Her Grace was not expected home at all. But if miss would wait in the morning room he would bring her tea.

Marjorie nervously sat down at a table by the window in the morning room and tried to will the minutes to go faster as a fat pot of tea cooled in front of her and the thin cucumber sandwiches slowly dried. She was so intent on her worries that she failed to hear the door opening. A slight cough from behind her made her swing around in her chair, nearly over-setting the tea tray.

"Philip!" she cried with shock and delight. Before she knew what she was doing, she had leapt to her feet and kissed him on the cheek.

And then turned as red as fire with embarrassment.

For the tall gentleman standing before her was not Philip. He certainly was as tall as Philip and had the same handsome face and tawny hair. But where Philip's eyes were blue, his were hazel, almost gold, with curved Oriental lids that gave his face an almost Oriental cast.

"I thought you were in France," said Marjorie, trying to recover her poise. The family likeness was strong and she realized this must be Philip's brother, the Marquess of Herterford.

"I am only back on a fleeting visit," he said in a light, amused voice. "I am Philip's brother, Robert, as you have guessed, but you have the advantage of me."

Marjorie shyly introduced herself and explained about the poetry reading.

The Marquess's thin eyebrows raised in surprise. "Philip! Poetry!" he exclaimed. "You must be joking."

"No, indeed," replied Marjorie anxiously. "He is very interested in poetry."

"Really? I would have thought 'The boy stood on the burning deck, his trousers were on fire' was about Philip's level."

Marjorie's eyes hardened. She decided she did not like Robert, Marquess of Herterford at all. He was callous, insensitive, and did not understand his brother.

"You do not understand your brother," she said, voicing the last of her thoughts aloud.

"Do you?" he mocked. "I wonder. I must rush to my next appointment, my dear, or I would stay to hear this fascinating recital."

He seemed to tower over her and she shrank back a little.

"But before I go," he went on, "let me return the compliment of your initial greeting." Before she could guess what he was about to do, he had leaned forward and kissed her on the cheek.

"How dare . . ." began Marjorie only to find that he had gone. Insufferable man! She hoped he stayed in France for the rest of his life and made no more "fleeting visits." What an irksome brother-in-law he would make. With her glove, she scrubbed her cheek where he had kissed her, wondering as she did so why she felt so breathless and upset.

The butler entered at that point to tell Miss Marjorie that Lord Philip had returned.

The poetry reading took place in a small salon on the ground floor of the house in Park Lane.

Joanna took her position at a small lectern and proceeded to declaim.

Marjorie's heart lifted. Why, her poetry didn't even *rhyme*. One didn't even grasp what the woman was *talking* about. The audience was composed of the crowd who had been at the river party. Lord Philip cleared his throat and explained that Miss Tyson had to leave them, and had any of them any poetry they would like to read? Trembling with nerves, Marjorie raised one pink-gloved hand and was rewarded by a rapturous smile from Lord Philip.

"Now, here's a surprise," cried Philip. "My lords, ladies and gentlemen, I give you Miss Marjorie Montmorency-James."

A vision in pink tulle, Marjorie walked nervously to the lecturn. She had not read the poetry she had written in the early hours before leaving her home. Now she wished she had.

But Marjorie was possessed of a great deal of courage. In a clear firm voice, she began to read.

" 'My Doggie,' by Marjorie Montmorency-James," she began, pleasurably aware that every eye was riveted on her.

> "I have a little Scottie dog
> His name is Mackintosh,
> He guards me in the London fog
> And barks, and all that tosh."

"Is that it?" asked Lord Philip in a curiously muffled voice.

"Oh, no," said Marjorie. "That was the end of *that* poem. I have others."

"*Do* go on," urged Philip, sitting down in his chair next to the lectern and putting a hand to his brow to shield his face.

So, much emboldened, Marjorie went on.

* * *

" 'The Sky at Evening.'
The sky at evening is pale and green and
lies o'er London city.
The day is done my dog is dead and that
is such a pity.
I weep and mourn and clutch my brow I
don't know what to do.
Till answer comes
     from the healing stars . . .
Buy yourself another dog.

  "I couldn't quite find a rhyme there," explained Marjorie with simple pride, "but I think the rest of it is not bad. Why, Hermione, I declare you are quite moved! There are tears in your eyes. Perhaps I had better not read any more . . ."

  "Oh, *do* go on!" chorused her audience.

  Marjorie blushed with pleasure and went on.

    " 'Lilacs.'
    I love the lovely lilacs
    So purple and so blue
    And when I see the lilacs
    It's then I think of you.

    "Their scent is sweet and heavy,
    They stand so tall and true,
    And when I smell the lilacs,
    My darling, I smell *you*."

* * *

Marjorie had meant to deliver the last line to Lord Philip but had not the courage. It seemed rather *fast* to do so.

"We have a special award for you," said Lord Philip, getting to his feet, his face strangely wooden. "Just wait there. Come along everyone. We'll all go to fetch Miss Montmorency-James's award."

After a polite applause, the company filed out, leaving Marjorie with stars in her eyes.

After the company and Lord Philip had shut themselves into a back study and laughed themselves silly, Lord Philip picked up a magnificent basket of roses and said, "We had better get back to our new poetess."

"But what's it all *about?*" demanded Mr. Lewis, already feeling disloyal at having laughed at Marjorie. "Yes, what's it all about?" chorused Toby while Guy Randolph and Lord Harry Belmont added their questions.

So Hermione told them.

To a man, the gentlemen were disappointed in Marjorie and thought her a very silly girl. They were disappointed, of course, because Marjorie had done it all for love of Lord Philip. Hermione was quick to point *that* out. Lord Philip still felt amused in a pleasurably malicious way. Anyone who wrote rubbish like that deserved all the ridicule in the world.

No one knew that Marjorie's pathetic silliness was caused by finding herself the center of attention in aristocratic circles, by being genuinely and deeply in love and by having been frozen in her early adolescence in the backwater of Haddon Common. She was still very much a schoolgirl.

Nonetheless, Lord Philip presented the basket of roses with great grace and charm and Marjorie left his house, her feet barely touching the ground.

It was the last she was to see of him for a whole seven days.

Although she assiduously visited the opera, Ascot, Goodwood and Henley and every fashionable ball and party in London, Lord Philip was unaccountably absent and her courtiers of the river party, strangely lukewarm.

She began to think Philip might be ill and at last sent a poem enquiring after his health to his home. It was a really terrible poem but somehow Marjorie's innocent love and yearning shone through the doggerel, and Lord Philip felt he had gone much too far and suffered pangs of conscience accordingly.

"It's not *your* fault," said Hermione to whom he unburdened himself. "She was simply *asking* for it. I can remove her interest from you for a breathing space if you would like. You can't go around missing the fun of the Season because she embarrasses you."

"How can you do that?"

Hermione tapped a silver pencil against

her teeth and frowned. "I'll think of something," she said, savoring with delight the renewal of their old closeness and friendship. "I'll find her someone else to emulate—someone, say, who belongs to one of those weird societies in Bloomsbury. That should keep her out of circulation for a bit. Shall I?"

Lord Philip hesitated. Something was wrong somewhere. He felt ill at ease and blamed Marjorie's pursuit of him for it. He had not been in the way of examining his own conscience and actions and he didn't feel like starting now.

"Oh, very well," he said languidly.

And with those three little words, he nearly killed Marjorie Montmorency-James.

Chapter Four

The weather blew hot and cold like Marjorie's fluctuating emotions. Her inflated ego had merely been a balloon balanced on the top of very little self-respect. Secretly, Marjorie did not think much of herself and was therefore liable to wild swings of mood, from elation where she felt like the prettiest girl in London to deep depression where she was plain Marjorie from the middle class—an upstart— with only her fortune to make her attractive to this glittering throng of loud-voiced, hard-eyed, self-assured people.

Fortunately for Hermione, Marjorie was in a depressed mood, six characters looking for an author, and ripe to hide what she felt was her colorless personality behind the role of emulating someone more interesting.

Her grandmother, Mrs. Wilton, and Lady Bywater had become engrossed in a series of bridge parties and for once Mrs. Wilton failed to notice that there was something the matter with her granddaughter.

Marjorie had been invited to go on a boating expedition on the Thames but the fickle English weather had made one of its abrupt changes and had decided to emulate a November day with all the skill of a Marjorie Montmorency-James.

The sky was low and leaden and a chill breeze scurried furtively through the London streets.

The boating expedition had been canceled, Lady Bywater and Mrs. Wilton were off at one of their bridge parties and Marjorie was left alone to sit and brood.

Why had *he* not replied to her poem? Marjorie paced restlessly up and down. There was a small shelf of books over in the corner and she studied the titles looking for something to pass the weary day. She at last drew out a slim volume, the poems of Elizabeth Barrett Browning. It had been ages since she had read any poetry other than her own. Miss Browning had written a poem to her dog, Flush, she noted. She began to read, "Therefore to this dog will I/Tenderly not scornfully/Render praise and favor." It was good, it was very, very good. A slow burning blush swept over Marjorie's pretty features. She rushed to the desk and drew out some of her own poems and scanned them hurriedly. They were simply awful! She must have been *mad*. Oh, God, how they must have laughed at her!

In the middle of all this mortification, the telephone rang in the hall. After a few seconds, Rose entered the drawing room. "Miss Hermione Ffofington on the instrument," she said primly as if Hermione were performing on the flute in the hall.

Marjorie gingerly picked up the earpiece and the heavy stand. Mrs. Wilton had not had the telephone installed at Haddon Common and it still seemed like a strange and unnatural device. "Are you there?" she said cautiously.

"Oh, Marjorie," came the brittle tones of Hermione. "Where *have* you been hiding yourself? You'll never guess what has happened. Philip has gone entirely *off* poetesses. He did say however that yours were jolly good . . ."

"He *did?*" gasped Marjorie. A great feeling of love for Hermione swept over her.

"Yes, he did. I say, are you all right? Your voice sounds jolly funny."

"No, I—I am perfectly all right. It was kind of you to call, Hermione."

"Not at all," came Hermione's disembodied voice. "Look, I have some simply fascinating news about Philip. I'm dying to tell you. Can I come round?"

"Of course," said Marjorie. "I would love to see you."

"Be with you in two shakes. Toodle-oo!" said Hermione cheerfully and rang off.

Marjorie returned to the drawing room and bravely rang for the butler and ordered tea. Lady Bywater's butler, Jenkins, was so elderly and imposing that Marjorie felt it was rather like commanding an archbishop to fetch tea.

Mackintosh came bounding into the room, his stubby tail beating a tattoo of pleasure on the carpet as he stared adoringly up at Marjorie with his leash in his mouth.

"No, I am *not* taking you for a walk, you silly thing," snapped Marjorie.

Mackintosh whimpered slightly and put his square muzzle dismally between his front paws.

Jenkins gave a discreet cough. "I am about to take the air, Miss Marjorie," he said, "and I would be delighted to take the little doggie with me. Rose may serve the tea."

"Thank you," said Marjorie, suddenly feeling shabby as Jenkins's austere face actually broke into a smile as he bent over Mackintosh.

"Are you coming a walk with me, Scottie? Are you? Good. Come along now!" Mackintosh picked up his leash and bounded after the butler, throwing a reproachful look over his shoulder at Marjorie.

A beautiful new life opened up for Mackintosh. Jenkins did not tug him impatiently along as his mistress did. Jenkins did not look embarrassed when he wanted to sniff at a particularly delicious lamppost. But most of all, Jenkins took him into that well-known servants' pub, The Duke of Clarence. Oh, bliss! There were footmen with poodles and butlers with corgis and spaniels and grooms with Yorkshire terriers, other Scotties and West Highlands. Jenkins and Mackintosh settled themselves in a cozy corner by the coal fire to enjoy the afternoon.

It was not that Marjorie was not an animal-lover. It was just that she was a Philip-lover and could not at that moment spare one ounce of feeling for anything or anybody else. True love is a peculiarly self-centered emotion and Marjorie was no different from anyone else.

She soon forgot her guilt over Mackintosh and settled down to wait for Hermione. She had not long to wait.

Hermione did not waste time on tea or preliminary social gambits but came straight to the point. "Before I tell you the news about Philip," she began, "you must promise me not to breathe a word to a soul. It is deadly secret."

Marjorie gave her word, her eyes like saucers.

"Philip," said Hermione in a low voice, "is a member of the Camden Town Anarchists!"

"But what are they?" asked Marjorie, bewildered.

"Oh, they are a nutty group of strange people who meet in a house in Camden Town and plan to overthrow the King and the government and . . . and . . . everything."

"But Philip would not have anything to do with that!" cried Marjorie.

"Oh, yes he has," said Hermione. "He told me they don't believe in every Tom, Dick or Harry having the vote. He says all the stuffy old establishments should be torn down so that they can rebuild Britain in their own image. Isn't it awful?"

"But," protested Marjorie with a rare flash of common sense, "Philip stands for everything that is old and stuffy, so to speak."

"He is bored," said Hermione. "That's all. This is merely something to alleviate the boredom. He enjoys danger and he says he is not interested in any woman who is not prepared to share that danger with him. He never goes to their meetings, he is one of their *most secret* members. But he says he won't have anything to do with me unless I go to their beastly meetings and learn all about the movement. And I can't and I won't. Then he said I hadn't any courage but he was sure there were women who had. I hate to lose him but I simply haven't got that kind of courage, dear Marjorie."

"Were . . . I mean are . . . you engaged to Lord Philip?" asked Marjorie, her voice barely a whisper.

"Not officially," said Hermione. "We always had an understanding but I'm not taking part in this lunacy."

"I didn't know you had an understanding with Lord Philip," said Marjorie accusingly. "You might have told me. Why did you encourage me to write that silly poetry?"

"It wasn't silly," cried Hermione. "The fact is that Philip was already growing cold toward me and I didn't want Amy or Jessie to have him. I've taken a liking to you, Marjorie. You're more sensitive than the sort of girls I know."

"Are you trying to tell me that *I* should join this group?" asked Marjorie.

"Oh, no!" shrieked Hermione in mock horror. "I simply had to have someone to confide in. I cried all last night."

"Where has Lord Philip been? Has he been working with these anarchists? Is that why I haven't seen him?"

Hermione nodded.

"It's too ridiculous," said Marjorie. "I can hardly believe it."

"It's true enough," said Hermione sadly. "If the police find out, Philip's going to be in awful trouble. I got as far as standing outside their headquarters. It's in a sleazy sort of place, number nineteen Peter Street in Camden Town. I didn't have the courage to go in."

"I am doing nothing today," said Marjorie thoughtfully. "Perhaps I might just go to see what the place looks like."

"Oh, you *mustn't*," cried Hermione, "I wish I hadn't told you." She pierced Marjorie with a well-feigned look of jealousy, which did more to convince Marjorie that the tale was true than anything that had gone before. "I really must leave now. You must promise me you will not do anything about this. Philip would never forgive me if he knew I had told you."

Marjorie replied with a noncommittal murmur and Hermione left, well satisfied.

Marjorie sat for a long time in thought after she had gone. It seemed that Lord Philip was not the god she had imagined. The Camden Town Anarchists indeed! Marjorie's adoration of Lord Philip was now strengthened by a new strong maternal feeling. At all costs, he mustn't come to harm. She, Marjorie Montmorency-James, would see to that!

A half hour later, dressed in a plain black coat and close-fitting hat borrowed from Rose, the parlormaid, with the excuse that Marjorie was attending a fancy dress tea as a maid, Marjorie cautiously set out to find a cab to take her to Camden Town. The nearest cab rank was deserted except for a four-wheeled clarence.

The clarence was more familiarly known as "the growler" because of the terrible noise it made as it rolled over stone or macadam roads. This one proved to be no exception. The loose rattling windows added a tremulous, shaky note to the growling bass of the wheels. Dirty straw littered the floor. The surly, overworked coachman was as decrepit as his horse.

Marjorie was jolted, deafened and rattled to bits by the time the ancient vehicle turned into the narrow and smelly confines of Peter Street.

The coachman charged her five shillings and Marjorie innocently paid. The fare should have been one shilling and sixpence.

"Look, miss," said the coachman, his sharp eyes having noticed Marjorie's expensive boots peeping out from beneath the shabby coat. "I have to rest me 'orse. Is you a-going to be long? For if not, I'll waits 'ere for you and take you home."

"Please wait, cabby," said Marjorie gratefully. "That is, I may be about half an hour."

"S'all right with me, lady."

Marjorie turned and surveyed number 19 Peter Street. It was a tall, narrow tenement with dirty curtains at the window. Peter Street was little more than a short cul-de-sac. The tottering buildings on either side of number 19 were deserted and empty.

The coachman voiced Marjorie's thought. "Sure you've got the right address, miss? Them buildings is condemned."

"I think so," said Marjorie doubtfully. Now that she had come all this way, she was reluctant to go back without finding out *something*. She shivered in Rose's thin coat. The sky was growing darker by the minute. A workman crossing the end of the street stared at her curiously.

Courageously, Marjorie walked up to the door. There were so many bells like a series of organ stops sticking out at the side of the door that Marjorie despaired of finding the right one. She peered at the names and then found one at the top that simply consisted of a grimy card with C.T.A. printed on it.

She took a deep breath and pulled the bell. There was a long silence.

Well, whoever it was would have to come all the way down the stairs to let her in. Behind her, the elderly cab horse wheezed and stamped and a lamplighter came along the street with his long brass pole to light the lamps.

Marjorie turned to watch him. Who could ever see a lamplighter go by without turning to watch? Like a magician, he raised his brass pole and immediately a gas flower burst into bloom. The air was now damp and misty and the lamp was a globe of light surrounded by concentric rainbows, a miniature Saturn in a dirty London world.

Marjorie turned back. Through the cracked glass of the door, she could see the wavering gleam of a candle as someone came downstairs.

The door was jerked open and a very hairy young man stood there. He had so much hair on his head and so much hair on his face that his small eyes peered out at Marjorie like some wild creature staring out of the underbrush.

"Yerse?" he demanded, holding the candle up and studying Marjorie's face.

"I have come to join you," she said in a low voice, in case the cabbie should hear.

"Garn!" said the young man rudely. "Go back to your ma."

"Go back to yours," snapped Marjorie, all of a sudden not at all scared, merely furious. "Because you badly need a wash."

"Hoity-toity," he said in an affected voice. "You'd better come in. Send the cab away."

"No," said Marjorie firmly. "I have merely come to join and to have a list of your meetings and then I'm leaving."

"Don't stand jawing on the doorstep, madam," he said sourly. "You want the whole bloody street to hear you?"

Marjorie stepped past him into the dark hallway, which smelled of cats and cabbage and urine, the age-old smell of poverty. There was a scuttling noise in the shadows.

"Rats!" said the young man behind her gleefully.

"Of course," said Marjorie coldly. "This place needs as much of a wash as you do."

He sniggered but moved past her to light her way up a rickety flight of stairs. Marjorie had reached that excited point of bravery known to many soldiers. She had charged into battle and all her fears had left her.

Higher and higher they climbed until he came to a stop outside an attic door and knocked three times. A Judas in the door cracked open and a dirty sharp female face looked through.

"Password," she demanded.

"Come on, Phyllis. It's me, Tony."

"Password," repeated the grimy female in more militant tones.

"All right, all right," sighed the young man. "Down with everything."

The door swung open and Marjorie found herself in a low-ceilinged room.

Apart from the female doorkeeper and the young man, there were four people, all men and all as wild and unkempt and hairy as Marjorie's escort. There was no furniture in the room and the company were seated on the bare boards before a smoky fire, drinking Wincarnis tonic wine. Marjorie wondered if the tonic wine was to fortify them for the revolution or if they had stolen it or could not afford anything else.

"She says she's a new member," said Marjorie's escort, jerking a thumb at her. Six pairs of eyes studied Marjorie.

"My name," said Marjorie's escort, "is Tony Byles. That there is Phyllis Sidebottom. On the floor from left to right is Joseph, Charlie, Bernie and Jim."

"How do you do," said Marjorie politely. They all seemed to find this very funny and screamed with laughter.

Phyllis was the first to recover. "How did you find out about us?" she demanded.

Marjorie did not want to mention Lord Philip's name since by doing so she would betray her friend Hermione. "In the newspapers," she ventured boldly.

To her relief, they all nodded. "That would be the *Camden Weekly*," said Phyllis proudly. "Blamed us for the bombing of the post office, it did, but the police couldn't prove nothing."

There was a silence while Marjorie digested this news about bombs. The anarchists must be very punctual people, she thought, noticing a row of brass alarm clocks along the mantelshelf.

"Why do you want to join us?" asked Tony at last.

Marjorie took a deep breath and repeated as much of what Hermione had told her as she could remember.

"Name?" said Phyllis, joining the interrogation.

"Rose Cummings," lied Marjorie, using the parlormaid's name.

"What d'you do?" chimed in Joseph.

"Parlormaid."

"OOOH!" they all screamed with mock gentility and began curtsying and bowing. "How refeened!"

"Shut up!" barked Tony, who seemed to be in charge. "Look here, Rose, you can't just come barging in here, demanding to join us. You'll need to take a test. Then we'll consider you."

Rose-Marjorie took a deep breath. "All right," she said.

"Make it a good un," shrilled Phyllis. Marjorie surveyed her with dislike. She was a small thin girl in a grubby purple silk dress. She had greasy hair of an indeterminate color scraped back in a bun and wore a pair of cracked elastic-sided boots. She smelled quite terrible and Marjorie wished she wouldn't move about so much. It was apt to spread the bouquet around the place.

There was a long silence while they all pondered Marjorie's fate. The sky outside the window was quite black and somewhere from below came the whickering of the cab horse.

"Got it!" cried Tony at last. "You know White's Club in St. James's Street?"

"I know *of* it," said Marjorie. "It is a gentlemen's club. Women are not allowed in."

"Nobody's asking you to go *in*," said Tony triumphantly. "Here's what you got to do. You've got to throw a brick through the window."

"What good will that do?" demanded Marjorie crossly.

"It will strike a blow at the heart of the establishment. You're to put a note on the brick saying it's a present from the anarchists, see. We'll move our headquarters tomorrer. We've got to get out of this place tonight, anyways. Give us your address and we'll send you word of our new place. If you do it."

"Look at 'er face," jeered Phyllis. "She'll never do it."

"Oh, yes I will," said Marjorie, feeling strangely calm. God would surely reward her with marriage to Lord Philip after all this devotion and courage. The Lord helps those who help themselves. Everyone knew that.

The company stared at her in amazement and admiration. Marjorie explained she was in service to a Mrs. Wilton who would most certainly not allow her to receive letters. She cringed at the thought of the real Rose receiving a letter from the anarchists. "One of you shall meet me at the Albert Memorial in Kensington Gardens," she said. "At three o'clock tomorrow."

This appealed to their plotting natures and they agreed but all surveyed her with mocking glances. They never thought for a minute that she would do it. She said:

"I believe a certain member of the aristocracy belongs to your organization." They looked at her rather blankly and then Tony said stoutly, "Of course. But we don't tell no names, see. We've got all sorts of grand folks on our list."

Tony received admiring nods from his friends. Like Tony, they were all rather impressed by the beautiful Marjorie and did not want her to think that she was meeting the sum total of the organization.

Marjorie was glad to escape outside into the cold open air. She was very thoughtful as the coachman rattled her back to the cab rank near Eaton Terrace. She would have to do it and do it that very evening before she lost this newfound calm courage. But White's, of all places!

Founded one year earlier than the Bank of England, White's is the oldest London club and the most famous in the world. In 1811, Beau Brummell and his friends had made the famous bow window their private preserve. Called once "an oasis of civilization in a desert of democracy," White's is the club with the most exclusive members list.

And one of its most exclusive members was Lord Philip Cavendish.

Marjorie paid off the coachman—another five shillings—and then looked up at him. "I would like to hire you for this evening," she said. "What is your name?"

"Charlie, miss," said the cabbie. "And my 'orse, he's Charlie too."

"I will pay you, let me see, two pounds to take me to White's Club in St. James's Street. You are to wait a few minutes for me. If you bring me back safely here," she indicated the cab rank, "then I will pay you another two pounds. But . . ." she went on as Charlie was about to express his willingness to drive her to the ends of the earth . . . "you must not tell anyone about me, no matter what happens."

"Cross my heart, miss," said Charlie fervently. Four pounds in all. Four whole pounds! There had been a cabbie only the other week who had jumped off Westminster Bridge because he couldn't stand the long hours and starvation any longer. Charlie, the horse, would have the biggest sack of oats he had ever seen and Charlie, the master, would have steak and kidney pie until it came out of his ears.

"I shall be here at eleven o'clock," said Marjorie, feeling very like a heroine in a novel. "Do not fail me."

"Not me, miss," said Charlie entering into the spirit of the thing. "No one shall 'ear a word from old Charlie, not if they were to torture him ever so."

Satisfied, Marjorie returned home, drawing the thin coat around her and skulking along in the shadows. She really must buy a cloak, she thought.

Lord Philip Cavendish did not believe in divine intervention. He was sitting in the famous bow window of White's staring at the club bore, General Arthur Hammer, as if he could not believe his ears. Indifferent to his glazed eyes, the General pontificated on the insanity of the Women's Suffragette Movement, the Cruel Sports League and the Bolshevists. The country was simply going to the dogs.

Democracy was a lot of rot. What England needed was to be governed by a few strong people like himself. Lord Philip had unwisely told the General he was awaiting the arrival of Toby Anstruther and so had neatly cut any line of retreat. The leather armchairs were deep and comfortable and his head began to nod. Oh, God, he thought wearily for the tenth time, let something happen to silence this incredible bore.

As if in answer to his prayer, there was a terrible shattering of glass as a brick sailed through the window and crashed onto the carpet between them.

"Bless my soul," cried the General.

Lord Philip jumped to his feet and stared through the shards of glass into St. James's Street. There were quite a number of carriages: hansoms, victorias, cabriolets, broughams and a shabby old clarence. There were startled shouts and yells and the club porter ran out on the steps and started shouting for the police.

Lord Philip ran out after him. A small crowd had gathered and was already noisily discussing the great event. It was the Suffragettes, the Bolshevists, the Cruel Sports League. They all sounded like so many General Hammers.

Lord Philip returned to the club to find General Hammer waving a piece of paper. "This was tied round the brick," he cried.

Lord Philip read the note. It said very simply, "A present from the Anarchists." The handwriting was educated and he felt sure that somehow he had seen it before. But that was impossible!

Charlie, the coachman, drove back to Belgravia in a thoughtful mood. Who would have thought such a nice young lady would do a thing like that? But four quid was four quid and he could almost taste that steak and kidney pie. Life was hard and he was damned if he would turn the best fare he had ever had in his life over to the police.

Marjorie descended from the four-wheeler and fastidiously brushed the straw from her skirt. Charlie breathed a sigh of relief when she handed over the four pounds. "I would like to engage you tomorrow," said Marjorie. "I wish you to drive me to the Albert Memorial, wait for me, and drive me back here. I will meet you at two-thirty. You will be paid well for your silence." Marjorie savored that bit about Charlie being paid well for his silence. It was just like something out of a book. She felt very proud of herself. She had neatly shied the brick straight through the bow window of White's without leaving the carriage. She had vaguely made out two men seated at the window but they were sitting opposite each other and well apart. She was sure she had not hurt anyone. She felt tremendously brave.

Charlie, the coachman, touched his hat. "Be glad to be of service to you anyhow, my lady," he said, elevating Marjorie to the ranks of the peerage. Marjorie nodded and pulled her coat collar up around her face and, with an absolutely unnecessarily furtive look around, glided off into the shadows.

It is amazing what good food will do for a man and his horse. Next day Charlie-the-coachman was wearing a large nosegay in his buttonhole and had washed his face and hands. Charlie-the-horse was almost frisky and stepped out smartly on the road to Kensington Gardens as if remembering better days.

The sun was shining and the gardens were a pretty oasis of green. The Albert Memorial, looking for all the world like a bit of a church that had become bored and wandered off on its own, pointed up to a pale blue sky. Marjorie was feeling tense and nervous and hanging onto her role for all she was worth. The papers had been full of the incident and Scotland Yard was quoted as saying it had put its best men on the job.

The names of the two men in the bow window had been withheld.

Tony was waiting eagerly for Marjorie. He too had washed to celebrate the occasion and looked twice as hairy. Marjorie led him round the far side of the memorial away from the watching eyes of Charlie, parked on the road.

"You have passed the test," said Tony, looking as pompous as a shabby young man with a lot of hair can manage to look. "Our new headquarters are in Burnham Road, Gospel Oak, number fourteen. Don't write it down! Should you be arrested, you must swear never to reveal our names."

"I swear," said Marjorie, feeling rather silly.

How mad it all seemed! The sun blazed down on the pretty dresses of the ladies strolling in the gardens, on the gold and red of the guardsmen's uniforms, on the frilly starched caps of the nursemaids. She no longer felt frightened. How could anyone take this comic opera group of anarchists seriously?

"Our next meeting is tomorrow at three o'clock," Tony was saying. "Then we'll let you know about our master plan."

"How nice," said Marjorie vaguely. She was to go to Jessie Wuthers's ball that evening. Perhaps Philip would be there.

"Here comes a copper," hissed Tony suddenly. "Try to act natural."

"I *am* acting naturally," said Marjorie with some asperity. "It's *you* who look shifty."

Really, thought Marjorie, this must be some sort of a game for Philip. He probably doesn't take it seriously either.

Both waited in silence until the policeman had passed. Then Marjorie said, poking nervously at the turf with the ivory point of her parasol, "If you will recall, I mentioned that I understood a certain member of the aristocracy to be part of your ... our ... group. Will he be at this meeting?"

Not for the world was Tony going to tell her that they did not boast such a distinguished member. "Not him," he said. "He works in the background, he does."

Marjorie frowned. "I happen to know the gentleman you mean," she said. "He sometimes calls on my mistress. Should I indicate to him that I too am a member?"

"No!" screamed Tony in alarm, and then in a lower voice, "No. He says no one must ever know 'cept me. You'd never guess he was one of us. He don't talk like us. But he's loyal just

the same. See here, if you go blabbing your mouth, we'll be in trouble."

Marjorie felt strangely disappointed in Philip. But perhaps he belonged to a higher echelon of the society.

"Where did you get those togs?" asked Tony suddenly. Marjorie was wearing a gown of mauve *mousseline de soie*. A wide organza hat held a whole garden of violets and her white kid gloves were smoothed over her arms like a second skin.

"Borrowed them from the missus," said Marjorie. "Oh, look! That policeman is coming back and he seems to be looking at you so strangely."

That was enough for Tony. He turned and ran.

Marjorie made her way back to the clarence deep in thought. She had no other part to play but the present one and she did not want to return to being plain Marjorie, a character she did not think much of at the moment.

She handed Charlie a five-pound note and walked away from the cab rank, still deep in thought. Charlie stared at the small fortune in his hands. "Hey, my lady!" he called after her. "Was you needin' me again?"

"What? Oh, yes, tomorrow . . . at two," replied Marjorie vaguely and turned and continued to walk away.

Charlie sat for a long time, clutching the

note. Oh, those Bank of England five-pound notes! Was there ever anything like them? Crisp and white and large, etched with a delicate scrollwork of black lines.

Charlie stretched his old arms up to the sky. He would . . . he would . . . By George! . . . he would take the rest of the day off. There was a pub he knew of, just a ways out on the Chiswick Road. Next to the pub was a meadow with long lush grass for the horse. Inside was a pretty barmaid behind the bar and pigeon pies *on* the bar. God bless the poor mad thing, he thought. I hopes my lady can afford it.

Marjorie indeed could, Mrs. Wilton having supplied her with a ridiculously large amount of pin money. She went through that day in a kind of bewildered daze. There was no Mackintosh to confide in, the little Scottie having transferred his affections to the bulter. Marjorie had gone down to the butler's pantry to look for him and had found Mackintosh sleeping off a large meal with his square black head pillowed on the butler's feet.

She still had a vague and dreamy look on her face as she entered the Wuthers ballroom. Her eyes looked black and enormous in her pale face. She wore a very low-cut gown of white silk, held on the shoulders by bows like wings. She looked very young and vulnerable. Philip with characteristic single-mindedness forgot completely about his discussion with Hermione, he forgot that Marjorie had ever irritated or embarrassed him, he even forgot that only the other night some anarchist had shied a brick at him. He headed straight across the ballroom floor and claimed Marjorie for the first waltz. He was very aware of his own hand pressed at her waist, aware of her scent, aware of her strange seductive appeal.

To his surprise, Marjorie said abruptly, "I want to talk to you. In private."

"Of course," said Philip smoothly. "There will be no one in the garden just now. We shall go there." He had not given any other man time to sign Marjorie's card and there was no other partner waiting for her.

They walked down a curving iron stair that led from the first floor to the sooty garden below. It was not a very romantic setting. A full moon, looking like someone with a bad case of smallpox, glared down. There was a sooty, scrubby patch of lawn, bordered by sooty marble figures firing arrows and holding urns and throwing discus—all sooty. There were a few sooty laurels and a few sooty pollarded trees. In fact, the whole garden smelled rather like the inside of a chimney.

"We daren't sit down," said Lord Philip, "or our clothes will be ruined. What do you want to talk to me about?"

"England," said Marjorie.

"*England?* You mean, this happy breed of

men, this little world-type England? This precious stone set in the silver sea-type England?"

"Yes."

"Oh, Marjorie," said Lord Philip in a husky voice. "Who are you trying to be now? You look so beautiful and you behave like such a ninny!"

Marjorie opened her mouth to protest and quite abruptly, he jerked her roughly into his arms and closed her mouth with his own. He forgot time and space and sooty gardens. Marjorie forgot the anarchists and the future of England. The world was narrowed down to this moment of heady passion as they kissed and kissed again until both were trembling.

He removed his white gloves and ran his long fingers caressingly over her neck. A cloud moved across the moon, plunging the garden into darkness. With a little groan, he slid his fingers into her hair and kissed her on the mouth again, slowly and lingeringly, teasing and caressing her mouth with his own.

"I love you, Marjorie," he said huskily, meaning, "I want you, Marjorie."

"I love you too, Philip," said Marjorie shyly. "Oh, Lady Bywater and grannie will be so pleased! They have always admired you and of course Lady Bywater is an old friend of your mother."

"So pleased about what?" he asked cautiously.

"About us!"

"About *us!*" Lord Philip heard the rattling of the cage door. What a fool he had been! He would find himself married if he did not extricate himself quickly. Making love to Marjorie was one thing, marrying her was another!

"You must not shock your grandmother by telling her of your amorous flirtations," he admonished. "She would be horrified. I did not behave like a gentleman, Marjorie, and for that I am truly sorry. What a scandalous pair we are! Let us go back to the ballroom quickly just as if nothing had happened."

The garden was still in darkness and so he could not see the look of extreme hurt in Marjorie's eyes.

"Come along now," he said, taking her arm in his. "Goodness, how dark it is! Watch your step. This staircase is quite treacherous. Up you go!"

The light from the ballroom shone full on Marjorie's face. She faced Lord Philip with a pathetic, hurt dignity. "Thank you for an interesting experience, Lord Philip," she said in a low voice. "We shall not speak of it again."

With a chilly nod of her head and a sort of half bow, she turned on her heel and left him standing.

At first he experienced a feeling of relief at having escaped so lightly. Then he saw her dancing some time later in the arms of Toby Anstruther. Toby was holding her much too closely and they went in to supper together.

And then Lord Philip discovered that of the two of them, it was perhaps Marjorie who had come off the lightest. He did not like himself at all. He felt like a cad. Actually he *was* a cad but it was a new and salutory experience for him to recognize the fact. He took Hermione in to supper and hardly heard a word she said.

Hermione made no reference to Marjorie and the anarchists. Marjorie had not mentioned anything about them to Hermione and Hermione assumed that Marjorie had not been mad enough to join them. Also Marjorie was looking at Lord Philip as if he were a species of slug so that was all right. She felt tremendously happy and completely untouched by Philip's moodiness. She was used to it after all and to tolerate it made her feel quite wifely.

Marjorie flirted with various young men who all seemed alike, patent leather hair, glossy faces and "ripping" this and "ripping" that. She wanted revenge. If she could find some definite proof that Philip was a member of the anarchists, then she would send it to the police. And . . . and . . . she would give herself up too and they would go to prison together. Oh, why was she so silly! She would be in the women's prison picking oakum, whatever that was. She hated him, she loved him and she wanted to go home.

"Another headache!" exclaimed Lady Bywater. "I declare us old things are running you off your feet, Marjorie. But I, for one, will be glad of an early night"—it was one in the morning—"and so will your grandmother."

Mrs. Wilton seemed disappointed at leaving the festivities so early. She had actually danced herself, and with *such* a charming gentleman called General Hammer.

Of the party that set out for Gospel Oak the next day, Marjorie was the only one who was out of spirits. Charlie-the-coachman had a new coat and so did Charlie-the-horse. Both seemed overjoyed to see her. Marjorie felt miserable. She slumped in the corner of the growler and stared out with unseeing eyes as they jolted and rattled and rumbled.

The sad fact was that Marjorie was still deeply in love with Lord Philip with all her emotions although her brain screamed at her that she was being silly.

He did not care for her at all. Worse than that, he must think her *fast*. The terrible tyranny of the class barrier reared itself in Marjorie's head. Perhaps to him it had been like philandering with a servant girl. And she had thought he had meant to marry her!

And, horrors, he knew it! He had backed away from her like a shying horse.

Number 14 Burnham Road, Gospel Oak, was little better than Peter Street. It lay in that section of north London near the bottom end of Hampstead Heath. The anarchists' flat proved to be in the basement this time. Phyllis had seen her arriving and popped her greasy head up the area steps to hail her. Phyllis did not seemed thrilled to see Marjorie but led the way into a damp room whose walls had inexpertly been painted a flaming red.

There was a certain tension in the air and the anarchists did not seem as harmless as they had before.

There were even chairs to sit on.

Tony pulled forward one of these and motioned Marjorie to sit down.

He turned to face the room. "Brothers and sisters," he said in a loud voice, "Rosie has proved she is worthy of belonging to our fellowship." With the exception of Phyllis, the others nodded. Phyllis thought sourly that Marjorie was much too finely dressed for a parlormaid. Her skirt and blouse were very plain but they were of expensive material and her jaunty little felt hat was a miracle of the milliner's art.

There was a rickety gate-legged table in the middle of the room, covered with a shabby velvet cloth. Tony walked solemnly toward it. "Rose, before we tell you our plans, we will show you our prize."

With the air of a painter unveiling his masterpiece, he whipped back the cloth.

Marjorie stared.

At first sight it looked like a cheap metal cashbox with the lid open. Marjorie rose to her feet and walked to the table and looked down. She had never seen a bomb before but somehow she knew exactly what it was.

Packed as neatly as a Fortnum and Mason picnic hamper were a cheap alarm clock, a pistol, several detonators. Cakes of dynamite were neatly arranged round the sides.

Hoping against hope that she might be wrong, she asked, "What is it?"

"A bomb, you eeejit," sneered Phyllis.

"Joseph made it," said Tony proudly. "Did his training in Ireland, he did."

Everyone except Marjorie began to clap and Joseph stood up and made them a bow.

"So you have a bomb," said Marjorie, trying to speak calmly. "What are you going to blow up?"

"Buckingham Palace," said Tony. "That's what!"

Marjorie suppressed a gulp. She was suddenly very frightened. These madmen were in earnest. She was suddenly sure that Hermione had tricked her. Now that she loved Lord Philip with all his faults and did not think of him as some sort of god, her brain seemed to clear, thoughts tumbling one over the other. Hermione telling her about the poetry reading and the air of suppressed excitement and mirth when they had given her the presentation. The coolness of her suitors, including Lord Philip, after that. Hermione!

Hermione had told her about these anarchists. Hermione was trying to make her look foolish.

The least she, Marjorie, could do was to learn as much as she possibly could. All this flashed through her brain in the space of a minute. Then she said:

"I don't see how you are going to get into the palace yard in the first place and it will not do much good to leave it outside."

"We're not going in," said Tony smugly. "It is."

He jerked his head and Phyllis went out of the room and shortly came back, carrying a familiar dress box. Marjorie recognized it. She patronized the establishment herself. It was one of the House of Frederic's dress boxes. Phyllis even had the ribbons and wrapping to go with it.

"Where did you get that?" asked Marjorie.

"Dustbin up the West End," said Tony laconically. "Phyllis was passing just as the maid was putting it out."

"The House of Frederic are Queen Alexandra's dressmakers," said Marjorie.

"Exactly. And that's where you come in,

Rose. You're the only one of us who can play the part. Joseph will help you down to the House of Frederic in Lower Grosvenor Street. You'll wear some of them fancy clothes you've got and Joseph will leave you on the pavement just a little way away from this Frederic place. You're to hail a hansom and tell him to take it to the palace."

"It'll never work," said Marjorie. "It'll be much too heavy."

"They'll never think to look inside till it's too late," said Tony. "They'll think it's heavy but the label will put them off. Some of them court dresses weigh a ton. Jewels and all."

Marjorie bit her lip. It was brilliant in its mad, childlike way. Of course, she would simply not turn up. But what if they washed and scrubbed Phyllis to look the part?

Phyllis was looking at her suspiciously. "How come you get so much time off?" she asked.

"My mistress is in Deauville—in France," said Marjorie. "There's nothing for us servants to do."

Phyllis was not well versed enough in the ways of high society to question why a lady would not take her servants to France with her. She relapsed into a sulky silence, biting her fingernails and looking jealously at Marjorie's clothes from out of the corner of her eye.

"I haven't got all *that* much time," added

Marjorie desperately. "The butler's very strict. It will rouse his suspicions if I stay out much longer.

"Very well," said Tony grandly. "We'll see you here same time tomorrow."

"When is this bomb to be delivered?" asked Marjorie.

"Tomorrer. We'll let you know tomorrow," said Tony slyly. "But first, you've got to do something for us tonight."

"Haven't I proved myself?" demanded Marjorie.

"Yerse," said Tony slowly, his voice alternating between a Cockney whine and a quite respectable lower-middle-class accent. "But Phyllis here, she says we don't know enough about you. You've got to have another test. What is it, Phyllis?"

Phyllis raised her malicious eyes from the social column of a grubby *Times*. "It says here," she said, "that some old tart called the Duchess of Dunster is giving a party on a boat on the Thames, just about Tower Bridge, for her eldest son, the Marquess of Herterford, who's been abroad and has come back for to help his daddy run the estates."

Philip's brother. Oh, merciful heavens! What did they want her to do?

"You're to weasel your way into this party," said Phyllis, relishing the look of dismay on Marjorie's face, "and you're to push this cove over the side."

"And if I don't?"

"Then you ain't one of us," sneered Phyllis.

"*You* couldn't do it," snapped Marjorie. "What have you done for this organization that's so great?"

"She blew up the post office at Camden Town," replied Tony.

"Oh," said Marjorie in a small voice. Three people had been killed in the blast, she remembered. Why, these people were *murderers*, downright murderers. She must get away.

"Very well, I'll do it," she lied, enjoying nonetheless the look of surprise on Phyllis's face.

"Rose is all right," said the one called Charlie. "She'll do."

"She's done enough," said Joseph.

"If she ain't going to do this test, then I'm leaving," said Phyllis, jumping into the center of the room and standing with her arms akimbo. There was a short silence. The men certainly didn't want Phyllis to leave. She cooked for them in a slapdash kind of way and supplied other pleasures. She was also very good at placing bombs in buildings.

"She's got to do it," said Tony.

"Very well," said Marjorie, heading for the door. "Read your papers tomorrow."

She sank into the growler with a sigh of relief as Charlie-the-coachman and Charlie-the-horse bore her homeward. She would never see those terrible anarchists again.

But once Marjorie was safely home and drinking tea and eating muffins, she realized that she had no actual information to give the police. What a splendid idea it would be if she could foil the plan at the very last minute. She would be a heroine! Then those terrible class barriers would not matter. Lord Philip would have to court her. All England, and perhaps even Scotland, would read about her. Would it be so bad to push Philip's brother off the boat? It might be just a little boat and she would, of course, find out first if he could swim.

She did not doubt for one moment that she was included on the guest list. Lady Bywater was the Duchess's friend and anyone who could call a Duchess "Crummers" must be a very close friend indeed.

She looked up as her grandmother and Lady Bywater came into the room. Both were very flushed and excited and Lady Bywater was positively chattering.

"My dear!" she was saying. "Hattie Trent is a *shark*. Did you notice how she *gloated* over her winnings? But we shall have our revenge tonight."

"It was not a ... er ... very *cheery* party," remarked Mrs. Wilton, stripping off her gloves and unskewering her hat and boldly using the latest slang word. "It is only a game, after all. Hattie is too intense."

"She took all our money," said Lady Bywater

testily. "Ah, Rose. More tea if you please. And I for one intend to win it all back tonight!"

"Aren't we going to the Duchess of Dunster's party?" asked Marjorie.

"Oh, dear," said Mrs. Wilton. "We quite forgot about you, darling. I fear you have no engagements for tonight. But you have been racketing around so much. A quiet evening at home will do you the world of good."

"Wasn't I asked?" wailed Marjorie.

Lady Bywater looked rather shifty. "Well, as a matter of fact, we *all* were . . . asked, that is. But you wouldn't have liked it at all, Marjorie, and that's really why I turned down the invitation. It's simply a small party on some draughty boat to welcome her son back, don't you know. A *tiny* boat, I believe. In fact, the whole thing will be rather like what one used to call a *rout*. Everyone pushes and shoves to shake hands with the guest of honor and then drinks and eats a little and then shoves and pushes to get out."

"Perhaps I could go on my own?" suggested Marjorie hopefully.

Lady Bywater raised her hands in horror. "After refusing the invitation? Unheard of!"

"If I had thought it would mean so much to you," chimed in Mrs. Wilton, "of course we would have taken you. But it's too late now. But as Lady Bywater says, you wouldn't enjoy it. The guest of honor is Lord Philip's elder brother and he's quite grim by all accounts

and doesn't care for women or parties or—"
here her voice dropped one shocked register—
"even cards!"

"Where was the party to be held?" asked
Marjorie.

"I wish you wouldn't keep on and on about
it," said Lady Bywater testily. She walked
over to the looking glass above the fireplace
and took down one of the invitations that
were wedged into the gilt frame of the looking
glass. "But there you are—see for yourself."

Marjorie looked down at the card. The party
was to be held on a tea clipper called the
Valiant, moored at Tower Bridge pier.

Mrs. Wilton and Lady Bywater immediately resumed their plans for the defeat of
Hattie at the card table and Marjorie slipped
the invitation into her reticule.

"I shall just go upstairs to my room," she
said when she could get a word in edgeways.
"Do not worry about me. I shall spend the
evening quietly at home."

"That's a good girl," said Mrs. Wilton
vaguely.

In the privacy of her room, Marjorie turned
the invitation card over and over in nervous
fingers. She would go! England expected every
woman to do her duty. But then the image of
the Marquess's face rose before her eyes. For
all he had kissed her, he had seemed quite
formidable. He was also very tall and strong
and had not looked at all like an invalid. But,

after all, Philip would be there. He *must* love her. This love she felt for him *must* be reciprocated. How brave he would think her when she revealed all.

Charlie was not at the cab rank that evening and the other cabbies stared at the sight of a young lady in full evening dress, unescorted, trying to hire a hansom to take her to Tower Bridge. The first one in the rank gladly volunteered to take up this splendid beauty.

Oh, the agony of getting into a hansom cab gracefully! First, you put your foot on a small iron step about eighteen inches above the ground and then, with an athletic pirouette, lodged your foot on the platform up above.

And it was a miracle if you didn't get your hat knocked off or your hair messed up by the overhanging reins or soiled your gown on the rim of the nearby wheel. Unaccustomed as she was to getting into hansoms, Marjorie performed the operation gracefully, drew down the blinds and settled back in the smelly darkness of the cab to plot.

Chapter Five

Robert, Marquess of Herterford, stood stiffly at the head of the gangplank to receive his mother's guests. He bitterly wished that he had followed his father the Duke's example and cultivated a dicky heart. At the very mention of a party, the Duke would clutch his chest and collapse into the nearest armchair. Once when one of these attacks had seemed genuine, the Marquess had fetched the doctor and returned with him, much to the Duke's consternation, since he was discovered esconced comfortably in an old leather armchair with a goblet of brandy at his elbow and his nose buried in a copy of the Pink 'Un. Since that time the Marquess had been convinced his father's heart was as sound as his own but his mother still believed every "attack" and allowed him to stay at home in the country.

At the corner of his vision, he was aware of Hermione Ffofington chattering with his younger brother. He did not know how Philip could tolerate the girl. She never had a good word to say for anyone.

Another party came on board and he shook gloved hands and murmured the usual things. Yes, he was glad to be back. No, France had not been too hot for the time of year. Yes, it was unfortunate his father could not attend.

"I think that must be the lot," he said at last, turning to his mother. She frowned. "Lady Plumb's party has not arrived yet. Give them a few moments."

A light summer breeze ruffled the muddy black waters of the Thames. Behind him on the deck, which was covered with a gay red-and-white-striped canopy, the band was playing Elgar's "Cockaigne" overture. Above the boat on one side loomed the squat Tudor majesty of the Tower of London. At the side, the cathedrallike towers of Tower Bridge.

The Marquess was five years older than his brother. There was a certain family likeness between the two. Both were tall and handsome with the same brown hair. But the marquess, in contrast to blue-eyed Philip, had hazel eyes, almost gold in some lights, with curved, elongated lids. His mouth was thinner and firmer than Lord Philip's and his face was very severe, with deep lines running down either side of his mouth.

He turned impatiently to his mother. "I think we ought to . . ." he began, when she interrupted him with, "That's Lady Plumb arriving now."

A splendid barouche pulled by two glossy and expensive horses rolled up to the foot of the gangplank. The Duchess was intent on the arrival of Lady Plumb and did not notice a shabby hansom that had halted on the far side of the barouche so that it was mostly screened from the ship. But the Marquess did.

He watched curiously as a very beautiful girl in a pink gown descended nimbly from the hansom and darted round the barouche to join the tail end of Lady Plumb's party, which consisted of Sir Edward and Lady Plumb and her two toothy daughters, and now the mysterious lady in pink.

"I think we have a gate-crasher, mama," murmured the Marquess. "The girl in pink."

The duchess peered down at the ascending party and said, "Oh, my stars and garters, it's Marjorie Montmorency-James. What *is* she doing here? She's Riddles's protégée, you know, Penelope Bywater. She's no gate-crasher because I invited the girl and Riddles and the girl's grandmama. But Riddles turned down the invitation, explaining that she simply had to go to a bridge party to get her revenge, which of course I *quite* understand. So infuriating when some society shark takes all your money and you get no chance of revenge so . . . Good evening, Lady Plumb, Sir Edward. How are the girls? Blooming as usual? Ah, Miss Montmorency-James.

"Where *is* Lady Bywater? And your grandmama? I thought they were going to be breathing heavily over the bridge tables this evening."

"I came with Lady Plumb's party," said Marjorie hurriedly. "Really," said the Duchess acidly, "it looked more as if you had *annexed* yourself."

Marjorie blushed with mortification. She had hoped by tagging onto the Plumb party to get on board without attracting attention. She looked miserably at her feet.

"I think you are mistaken, mama," said a warm, deep voice. "I remember Lady Plumb said something about a Miss Montmorency-James joining their party."

Marjorie looked up at the Marquess in quick gratitude. "My dear, I *am* sorry," said the Duchess. "Robert will tell you I always jump to the worst conclusions. Now I must join the guests. Robert, do take Miss Montmorency-James to the buffet and then you really must speak to people, you know. You should be a bit more like Philip. *He* speaks to anyone."

"Depending on their class, of course," murmured Robert but his mother was already out of earshot.

Marjorie surveyed her rescuer. He was more tanned and fitter looking than when she had last seen him. The intense amused stare of his eyes were making her feel nervous. "I remember," he said softly, "we met before."

"Urch," mumbled Marjorie.

Now that she had met the Marquess again, she could not envision herself pushing him overboard. He was such a tall, powerful-looking man, she would probably bounce off him. She was anxious to escape and find Philip. She must tell him about the anarchists' plot and ask his advice.

But as Robert led her away, Philip looked up and saw Marjorie. A faint embarrassed flush mounted to his cheekbones and he looked quickly away. Hermione smiled sweetly at Marjorie and then turned to Lord Philip and laid a possessive hand on his arm.

Robert noticed this bit of byplay and mentally shrugged.

He was used to the role of consoling Philip's broken-hearted *amours*. Not that Philip ever went in for anything serious when it came to debutantes; he merely flirted, but he did seem to have a devastating effect on the poor things, thought Robert wryly.

Marjorie could not see how she could possibly get rid of this tenacious Marquess. He led her to the buffet, he filled her plate, he found a small table in a corner of the deck—if decks can be said to have corners—and then he watched her curiously as she shoved some of the most beautiful delicacies in the world around her plate. For a short time, his attention was distracted as one guest after another came up to welcome him home.

Marjorie made a little crabwise, shuffling movement in her seat at one time when she thought his attention was fully occupied but his head had jerked round and she had found herself mesmerized by that amused golden stare.

At last the other guests were settled at their respective tables. The band was playing "Poor Wandering One" and a light breeze from the river wafted all the expensive smells of cigar smoke, fine wine, lobster and game, and Atkinson's Lavender Water past Marjorie's jaded little nose.

"Aren't you going to eat or say anything?" asked the Marquess at last. "You haven't even commented on the weather."

"Very mild for the time of year," said Marjorie dismally. What nauseating great amounts of food they gave you! What lousy lobster, what tiresome ptarmigan, what bloody Beluga caviar!

Robert studied the dismal face opposite. She was indeed a very pretty girl, he reflected, with those strange eyes like the North

Sea. Her hair was teased out over her brow in a light brown cloud. Her pink dress displayed a modest amount of tantalizing bosom and her waist must only have been about nineteen inches.

It was a new experience for Robert to be so completely ignored. He detested parties himself but after all, he *was* the guest of honor and this little chit was receiving a lot of envious glances.

"Why did you gate-crash?" he asked, hoping to goad her into some sort of animation.

"I didn't really," said Marjorie politely. "I *was* invited. Only, grandmama and Lady Bywater wanted to play cards instead and an evening at home seemed tedious and so . . . and so . . . I came."

"It won't do, you know," he said gently. "I don't really think that moping over your food will attract Philip's attention. Also, it is very rude."

"Sorry," mumbled Marjorie, although underneath she was suddenly furious with hurt and embarrassment. How dare Philip snub her! How dare this terrifying brother of his sit here and lecture her. Why, he deserved to be pushed in the Thames. In fact, she had a jolly good mind to . . ."

Marjorie hurriedly picked up her role of anarchist-conspirator and put it on.

The Marquess blinked.

One minute, there had been a pretty but

sulky young thing opposite. The next, a handsome woman with commanding eyes—or
rather that was the impression she gave.

"How did you enjoy your stay in France?"
demanded this new Marjorie.

"Very much," he said, masking his surprise. "I was there for my health, you see, so I
stayed at a villa in Trouville and did not go
about much."

"What was the matter with you?" pursued
this new Marjorie, drinking wine with gay
abandon.

He considered the question very bad form
but nonetheless replied, "Pneumonia. I re-
covered but it left me very weak. The doctor
prescribed fresh air and sea bathing. It seemed
to do the trick although Trouville was deadly
dull."

Marjorie felt the wine hitting the bottom of
her stomach and then exploding up to her
brain in a series of golden skyrockets. She
gave her empty glass an impatient little push
and a waiter promptly refilled it. The Marquess began to feel uneasy. A little wine for a
girl of Marjorie's age was in order but not
great whole flagons of the stuff! It did not
seem to affect her much, he admitted to himself, unaware of the merry bacchanalia riot-
ing around the inside of Marjorie's skull.

Marjorie glanced across the deck and her
face hardened. Philip and a very pretty young
girl were sitting close together on one side of

the table for four. On the other side was
Hermione with Toby Anstruther. As Marjorie
watched, Philip took the pretty girl's hand
below the table and gave it a squeeze.

Marjorie's eyes were now wide and silvery
and she gave the Marquess her whole attention for the first time. "I am very flattered,"
she said, "to be entertained by the guest of
honor."

Her long black lashes dropped to her cheeks.
She's flirting with me, thought the Marquess.
She really must have a terrible pash for
Philip.

The Duchess glared across at her eldest
son. It was really too bad of Robert to monop-
olize that girl. He had had plenty of time to
eat and now he ought to be circulating among
the guests.

"Pink becomes you," Robert was saying,
enjoying the play of those fantastic lashes.
She must be the only female at the party who
did not smother her face with white enamel,
he thought.

"Thank you," murmured Marjorie, looking
full into his eyes.

The Marquess glanced out of the corner of
his eye at his brother. Marjorie now had
Philip's full attention. He was glaring across
at the pair of them.

"Good!" thought Robert. "Let's see if I can
make old Philip any more jealous."

Aloud he said, "Let me take you on a tour

of the ship, Miss Montmorency-James." Marjorie dutifully rose to her feet but as they left the deck on which the buffet dinner was being served, she began to feel conspicuous. No one else had risen and several startled faces were turned in their direction.

But the Marquess was almost urging her up the companionway to the deserted afterdeck. Marjorie stumbled as the full effect of all the wine she had drunk began to hit her. He grasped her arm to steady her and felt her tremble against him. Marjorie was not trembling with passion. She was trembling with fear. The opportunity was too good to miss. "Oh!" she thought drunkenly, "I will do it for England. I will save the Queen. Philip must love me! He must be made to."

The Marquess was standing at the rail. He had released her arm. She stood a little back, a little behind him. For a brief second, a cold sober breath of sanity seemed to blow through her brain. But then the mists of alcohol closed down. An eighteen-year-old girl often wavers between the woman and the child, between maturity and immaturity. When the eighteen-year-old is drunk, then the child takes complete control and fantasies become reality.

Marjorie gave the Marquess of Herterford an almighty shove right in the center of his elegantly tailored back. Instead of shooting over the rail as she had intended, he staggered slightly forward, grasped the rail firmly and heaved back with such momentum that he cannoned into her and sent her flying across the deck.

It was all too much for Marjorie. In the first place, her twenty-one-inch waist had been lashed down to nineteen by her corset, she was tipsy, she was frightened and Philip did not love her. She fainted dead away.

The only witness to the incident was Tony who waited in the shadows of the quay like a very hairy rat. He was quite satisfied. No one could say she hadn't tried. He knew she would not be arrested. Society never liked a fuss.

Marjorie slowly came out of a deep swoon. She was lying on a narrow bed and the bed seemed to be moving gently up and down. After a few seconds memory came flooding back. She was still on the boat. She was in a cabin on the boat and seated on a hard chair near the bed was the Marquess. At the door stood a stern-looking maid.

"Give her some brandy, my lord," suggested the maid, "She's coming round."

"She's had enough to drink," said the Marquess. "A cup of tea with a lot of milk and sugar will be much better. Now, Miss Montmerency-James, not one word until you have drunk your tea."

Marjorie eased herself up on the pillows

and stared at him miserably. Her mouth felt hot and dry and her head ached. She gratefully drank the hot tea.

"Where is Philip?" she asked plaintively.

"Philip and the rest of them have only been told that you fainted—not that you had tried to push me over. But now, Miss Montmorency-James," he went on, taking the teacup from her and placing it on a table with a peremptory little click, "you are going to tell me exactly why you assaulted me."

And so she did. She told him of Hermione's story about Philip being a member of the Anarchist party and how she had joined. She did not have the courage to tell him about throwing the brick. She told him about the plot to blow up Buckingham Palace and how she hoped to foil it.

As the Marquess listened to her, the harsh lines on his face softened and the stern maid at the door had tears in her eyes.

"I shall go there tomorrow—you know, to the headquarters in Gospel Oak," said Marjorie eagerly, now that she had apparently a sympathetic audience. "And ... and ... you shall tell the police and they can come at three o'clock and arrest them all.

"Oh, I meant to see this thing through to the end so that I could deliver their exact plans to the police, but I really can't go on. It is such a relief to tell *someone*."

The Marquess held out his hand and said gently, "Come, you shall wash your face with cold water and then I will take you home."

He helped her from the bed and led her across the cabin and opened the door of a surprisingly well-equipped bathroom. The tea clipper no longer ferried tea but had been converted to a yacht by a friend of the Duchess.

When the door closed behind her, the maid burst out crying. "It's terrible, my lord," she wept. "Such a pretty little thing to have all them mad ideas!"

"It's a tragedy," agreed the Marquess solemnly. "Hermione Ffofington made up some story about Philip and this poor girl believed it and dreamt the rest. There was a brick thrown through the windows of White's with a label tied to it saying it was a present from the anarchists. It was in all the papers. She probably read it and dreamt the rest. Poor, poor child. As if anyone in this day and age would try to blow up Buckingham Palace! Shhhhh! She's coming back."

The maid quickly dried her tears and bustled after Marjorie as the Marquess led her out. He led her away from the lights and music of the party. He talked of conversational nothings on the road home and the maid seated in the carriage opposite the Marquess and Marjorie could only admire his aplomb.

"Will you remember," she said shyly, "the address is number fourteen, Burnham Road, Gospel Oak. At three o'clock."

"Yes, yes," he said soothingly. "Now go to bed like a good girl and get some sleep."

Marjorie went to bed that night feeling as if a weight had been lifted from her mind. Once it was all over, she would call on Hermione and give her a piece of her mind. How could she, Marjorie, have ever believed dear Philip could have been associated with such a lot of crazy people as the Camden Town Anarchists!

In the broad light of a sunny new day, Marjorie's spirits were completely restored. Charlie-the-coachman and Charlie-the-horse were waiting for her at the cab rank. But after they had driven a little way, the growler rattled to a halt and Charlie climbed down heavily from the box and went round and opened the carriage door. He held out ten new pound notes to Marjorie and said urgently, "Here take this, miss!"

"I couldn't," said Marjorie amazed. "What is it for?"

Charlie went a deep red. "Well, it's like this, miss," he said awkwardly. "I've bin overcharging you. But I was so hungry and so was pore old Charlie there, that I took it. That there five-pound note you gave me, miss, I took it down to Ascot. There was this 'orse called Lilac Lady a-running at one hundred to one and the name reminded me of you seein' as how you wore a lilac dress oncet. I felt I had bin a-cheatin' of you and if the good Lord saw fit, why He'd make me lose. It cum in, furst. So I'm goin' to retire and Charlie there, he's goin' to retire and it's all on account o' you.

"An' see here, I wrote down the cab fares what they oughter be so you ain't goin' to get cheated agin."

"Please keep the money," said Marjorie with a touch of the role of anarchist-conspirator. "I was paying you for Extraordinary Services."

"Yerse, well that is what I wanted to talk to you about," said Charlie. "If you wants to shy bricks at gentlemen's clubs that's all right with me but don't yer ma know yer out? I mean ter say, you'll end in the pokey."

"It's all right," said Marjorie hurriedly, anxious to get to her destination. "All that's over and done with. You needn't wait for me today. A gentleman," here she saw the look on Charlie's face and hurriedly added, "a *very respectable* gentleman will be escorting me home."

"All right, miss," said Charlie reluctantly. He gave Marjorie an anxious look and climbed back into the box.

Marjorie looked at the watch pinned to her bosom. She hoped she would be on time. She did not want to tell Charlie to move faster. She didn't want old Charlie-the-horse to die before he had enjoyed his retirement.

But Charlie deposited her in Burnham Road exactly at three o'clock. "No fare, my lady," he said, smiling down at her. "Just 'eartfelt thanks from me and the 'orse. I'm a-thinkin' of goin' down to the seaside for to retire, see. Somewheres not too classy."

"Go to Sandypoint," said Marjorie, although most of her mind was on the anarchists. "That's a pleasant little spot and I believe the rents are moderate."

Charlie touched his hat and the growler rattled off.

Marjorie looked up and down the street. No one. Of course, the police must be hiding in some of the buildings.

"Come along," said Phyllis's acid voice from the area steps. "You going to stand there all day?"

Marjorie followed her down into the red-painted room. With a sinking heart, she saw the House of Frederic box with its pretty ribbons all parceled up and ready.

A new Tony was standing beside it. He was wearing a moderately smart suit and his hair and beard were neatly trimmed.

"So when do you plan to deliver the bomb?" asked Marjorie brightly.

Tony produced a pistol from behind his back and pointed it straight at Marjorie's heart.

"Today, Miss Montmorency-James," he said. "Today!"

Chapter Six

There was a long silence in the room. Marjorie turned very white. Phyllis watched her face avidly. Joseph, Charlie, Bernie and Jim stared at her coldly. They didn't look funny or silly at all. They looked like killers.

"Yerse, that surprised you," sneered Tony. "Oh, I saw you trying to push my lord off the boat. But I crept back just to make sure you didn't need any help. So what do I see? I see you and my lord leave that there boat all chatty and cozy. So I followed you. And this morning I asks around the servants in your manor and learns that Mrs. Wilton is your grannie, not your employer. So, I thinks, we've got one of these here debs looking for excitement. So you're going to get it. You and me are going to deliver this here package to Buckingham Palace in person. You look the part. Phyllis don't. We tried cleaning her up but it didn't do."

Phyllis, looking as dirty as ever, scowled malevolently.

"See," went on Tony, the pistol in his hand never wavering, "we decided to make sure it got there. Now if we sent it in one of them shabby hansoms, we'd never get it past the gates. What we need is a classy carriage and a fine-looking lady and we've got both."

A rattling on the cobbles outside diverted him. The police, thought Marjorie, weak with terror. Oh, thank God!

"That'll be our carriage now," said Tony, shattering her hopes. "Move!"

"But I can identify you all!" cried Marjorie. "You will shoot me anyway!"

"Oh, no," smiled Tony, "You're to be left alive with the mess. We want the world to know it was us what done it."

His eyes were fever-bright and Marjorie realized for the first time that he was completely and utterly mad.

He moved forward and dug the pistol into her corset.

"Move!" he said grimly.

He caught up a light coat from a chair and draped it over his arm to hide the pistol. Joseph and Charlie picked up the box.

A smart, rented brougham was stationed

outside. Marjorie looked appealingly at the driver but he was staring woodenly in front of him. The package was loaded into the brougham and Marjorie was prodded in after it.

Still hoping that the police might arrive, she stared eagerly out of the window.

No one!

And then she realized the Marquess had not believed a word of it.

Marjorie was very young, very immature, but she had more courage than most. She leaned her head back against the squabs, her face very white. She knew what she had to do even if it meant losing her life. The package must never be delivered.

What a long, long way it seemed to be until at last they turned into the Mall and clattered along under the plane trees. Tony had been mercifully quiet the whole journey.

The palace guards stood like toy soldiers and just about as caring. The carriage clattered into the palace yard—and was stopped.

Marjorie looked out of the window into the thin sharp face of a British bobby. There was a policeman on Tony's side of the carriage too. Both doors were simultaneously opened.

"What's this 'ere?" demanded the heavy voice of the law.

"Package from the House of Frederic for

Her Majesty," said Tony, staring straight ahead.

"Don't know you, mate," said the policeman. "Name?"

"Charles Percival-Smythe," said Tony promptly.

The sharp official eyes rested on Tony's smart clothes, then on Marjorie's white face, then back again to Tony, and then dropped to Tony's boots and rested there for a long moment.

Tony had forgotten about his boots. They were scuffed and cracked.

"Out! Both of you," ordered the policeman on Tony's side.

Marjorie tried to get out of her side of the carriage but Tony dug the gun into her ribs and so she followed him out on his side.

The two policemen faced them. "You come from this House of Frederic?" called one up to the driver.

"Not me, guv," said the driver. "Picked 'em up at Burnham Road, Gospel Oak. Hired me from Jones's Livery Stables, they did."

Marjorie sensed rather than felt Tony's arm move.

She knew he was going to shoot the policemen.

"He's got a gun!" she shouted and threw herself in front of the policemen.

"Bitch!" screamed Tony and shot at her point blank.

She felt a terrible impact and fell to the ground. Tony scampered out of the palace yard with the shrill sound of the police whistle sounding in his ears. Policemen seemed to blossom from every corner. The guards outside fired wildly as Tony plunged into St. James's Park. Fear lent his feet wings. Luckily for him, the park was fairly deserted—for everyone who *was* there from old men to small children and nursemaids tried to stop his flight. How he made it through Downing Street is a miracle but when he erupted into Northumberland Avenue with the No. 10 Downing Street police joining in the chase, he found it was congested with traffic.

He plunged into the traffic, trying to zigzag his way across. But distorted news flew with him. *"He's killed the King! He's killed the King!"* cried voices all around.

He had dropped his coat and his gun in the chase. Whips lashed down on his shoulders. Horses reared and plunged. A woman with a scream like a banshee went on and on.

A large Clydesdale pulling a coal cart reared up in fright. And the last thing Tony the anarchist knew on this earth was the crashing descent of those enormous hoofs.

At least, thought the police gathered in the palace yard, they had one alive to tell the tale.

The bullet had crashed into the steel of Marjorie's corset and had broken her ribs.

That latest piece of underwear designed to produce a Gibson girl figure had saved her life.

The appearance of Miss Montmorency-James in the magistrates' court was jam for the press. The small court was crowded to overflowing and prominent among the distinguished guests were Miss Hermione Ffofington, Lord Philip Cavendish, Tony Anstruther, Amy Featherington, Jessie Wuthers, Jeffrey Lewis, Mr. Guy Randolph and Lord Harry Belmont. The rest of the anarchists had disappeared as if into thin air.

Marjorie was numb with misery. She had spent a night in the cells and no amount of frantic string-pulling by Lady Bywater and Mrs. Wilton had been able to get her out of them.

Lord Philip felt uneasy. It had seemed like such a splendid joke when Hermione Ffofington had told him the lunacy of Marjorie's devotion. Now, here he was with his friends, chattering and laughing, and there in the well of the court was a pale and drawn Marjorie. "I can't stand this," he muttered to Hermione. "I want to go."

"Don't be silly," she whispered. "The fun is just beginning."

"Fun?" he thought, looking at her curiously.

The hearing began.

Now Hermione was not a particularly

wicked or cruel girl. It was just that her place in society and a certain insensitivity had insulated her from the harsher side of life. She wanted Marjorie convicted. The fact that the girl would be at least sentenced to a lifetime of hard labor did not cross her mind.

Marjorie was asked whether she would accept the judgment of this court or be tried at a higher court before a judge and jury. In a barely audible voice she said she would accept the judgment of the magistrates' court.

Then things began to go very wrong for Hermione as the evidence was read out. Marjorie had indeed told the whole truth and nothing but the truth in her statement.

All was revealed. Her love for Philip, Hermione's prompting her to join the anarchists, her desire to save England. She had not, however, admitted to throwing the brick into White's.

Then the policemen at the palace gave evidence that the girl had risked her life to save theirs. Then there was a peculiar character witness, a big old cabbie called Charlie who swore Marjorie was an angel. Then a surprise witness was called. His lordship, The Most Noble Marquess of Herterford took the witness stand while the press leaned forward eagerly and Philip suddenly wished he were dead.

The Marquess looked an awesome and commanding figure. He was tailored to perfection and his tawny hair shone in the dim light of the court. His strangely hypnotic stare seemed to mesmerize the court as he related in a clear resonant voice of how Marjorie had told him the whole affair and that he had not reported it to the police because he thought the girl was mad. He added wryly that his brother, Philip, had a devastating effect on the hearts of impressionable debutantes and that the whole thing had been prompted by malice on the part of a certain Miss Ffofington who, he believed, was also in love with his brother.

Hermione turned as white as Marjorie.

The Marquess went on smoothly. Miss Montmorency-James, he went on, was indeed a silly girl in one way. But he urged the court to admire her incredible courage. One or two policemen would be lying dead had it not been for her bravery. Had she not stuck it out to the last minute, then the anarchists would merely have killed her and tried again. Marjorie's defense lawyer rubbed his hands in glee. My lord was doing a splendid job.

"My lords, ladies and gentlemen," said the Marquess, his deep voice carrying to every corner of the overcrowded court. "I ask you to picture the dilemma of this young girl. She joins this organization under the mistaken impression that the man she loves is also a member of it. Having at last decided he is not, she does not shirk her duty. Picture that ride to Buckingham Palace! Picture the agony of a young girl who has led a sheltered life, forced to sit there with a pistol pressed into her side and a bomb at her feet. Does she faint or cry out? No! She puts her life in jeopardy for the safety of Their Majesties. Such a girl is the flower of English womanhood!"

Wild applause in the court from everyone but Marjorie's former friends who sat in white-faced silence.

"Since Miss Ffofington is, I see, in court," said the Marquess, "I think she should take the stand and explain how the whole affair began."

Hermione could have killed him, could have killed Marjorie. She made a very bad impression. She tried to laugh it off and her laughter rang shrilly in the silent court. Made worse by fear, she told of the poetry reading and by trying to make Marjorie look silly, she made herself appear a sort of Lady Macbeth.

Then Lady Bywater took the stand. Miss Montmorency-James, she said in repressive tones, was a thoroughly nice middle-class girl who had had her head turned by a certain irresponsible element of British society. It was her first Season and it was unfortunate that she had been made the butt of some feckless young things' practical joke.

After Lady Bywater, there was the evidence that the "cakes of dynamite" in the bomb were in fact cakes of shoe blacking. "Poor Tony," thought Marjorie irrationally. "He never could do anything right."

When she stood up to hear her sentence, she felt drained and tired. She really did not care what they did to her now. Her love for Philip seemed like a sick madness. With that gone, nothing else mattered.

It was some time before she could take in the wild cheering in the court, which spread to the waiting crowds in the street outside.

She was acquitted! The magistrate gave her a severe reprimand but nonetheless commended her bravery. He talked at length about the malicious and dangerous elements of London society who were prepared to ruin a life for the sake of a practical joke. He cited the case of Mary Abernethy who had been haunted the year before at Lord Glenwood's country home as part of a practical joke and who had died of fright as a result of it.

He reminded the court that Miss Ffofington and Lord Philip Cavendish had been members of that house party.

Marjorie Montmorency-James walked from the court a free woman. She had all the fame she had dreamt of, all the adulation.

And she didn't want a bit of it.

For the first time in her life, she wanted to play the role of Marjorie and never, ever try to be anyone else again.

* * *

The last trunk was corded, the last wicker hamper strapped down as the household in Eaton Terrace waited for the arrival of the Great Eastern Railway omnibus. Marjorie was going to Sandypoint.

Four days had passed since the trial and the household had known no peace. Letters for Marjorie arrived by the sackload. She could not leave the house even for a moment without being besieged by reporters and the adoring public.

"Get her out of town," Lady Bywater had ordered.

Mrs. Wilton, very subdued, very tired, very unlike her usual bustling self, was feeling her age as she carefully counted all the trunks and hampers for the umpteenth time. She had suggested Sandypoint because it was a quiet coastal backwater. It was full of elderly ladies like herself, a sort of Haddon Common by-the-sea.

Marjorie would have agreed to anything that removed her from the staring gaze of curious London. Oh, the misery of having her pathetic adoration for Lord Philip made public!

The three ladies were wearing their largest hats so that they would not be crushed on the journey.

There came a peremptory rap at the street door and Mrs. Wilton sighed with relief. "That will be the omnibus, Jenkins," she said. Lady Bywater's carriage was to take Mrs. Wilton and Marjorie to the station while the servants and trunks piled into the omnibus.

But it was Lord Philip Cavendish who stood on the step, looking very pale and handsome, his silk top hat held in his hands.

"Good afternoon, madam," he said, addressing Mrs. Wilton although he never took his eyes off Marjorie. "I would like a brief word in private with Miss Montmorency-James."

"Well, *really,*" said Mrs. Wilton bristling. "I think Marjorie has endured enough!"

"Oh, let him have his say," said Lady Bywater wearily. "And then let us thankfully close this most distressing chapter."

Mrs. Wilton reluctantly gave her permission.

Marjorie was too surprised to protest. She quietly led Lord Philip to the back study and stood facing him among the shrouded furniture. The day had turned gray and cold and a wind moaned in the fireless chimney.

"Well, my lord?" said Marjorie calmly.

Lord Philip did not know quite how to begin. She looked much older, much more composed. He had suffered at the hands of the press and the public. He had been lampooned as a "masher." He had never been unpopular in his charmed life and he felt he could not stand one more day of it. He had callously informed Hermione that the only thing he could do to allay public feeling was to marry Marjorie. To his horror, Hermione had burst into tears and threatened to sue him for breach of promise. He had not stayed to dry her tears but had presented himself at Eaton Terrace as soon as he could.

He smiled winningly at Marjorie and took her hand. "I feel I have behaved so badly," he said in a low voice. "Can you forgive me?"

Marjorie removed her hand. "It is not a question of forgiving you, my lord," she replied in a dead voice. "I am concentrating at the moment on forgiving myself."

"But we . . . I . . . was very cruel," he went on intensely. How pretty she looked! It might not be so bad after all. He took a deep breath. "Marjorie," he said, "I wish you to become my wife."

"No," said Miss Montmorency-James. "Why don't you ask Hermione? You are well suited."

He masked a feeling of irritation. "Ah, you *are* angry," he said, moving closer to her and trying to take her in his arms. "But there was a certain evening, if you remember, when you were not so cold to me."

Marjorie's eyes were as flat as steel. "I am also trying to forget that sordid little episode," she said in measured tones. She put out her hand and rang the bell.

"Jenkins, Lord Philip is just leaving. Good day to you, my lord. We shall not meet again."

It was then that Lord Philip Cavendish realized to his horror that he really loved her and wanted her.

"I say, Marjorie . . ." he began desperately but Lady Bywater appeared behind the butler's shoulder, her eyes quickly scanning Marjorie's face.

"You must excuse me, Lord Philip," she said, "but the carriage is waiting. Come, Marjorie. I shall be following you after all. Mrs. Wilton tells me there are marvelous card parties there! Lord Philip, I do urge you to remember that Marjorie's destination must be kept secret. The editors of the papers have agreed, with the exception of that Liberal rag, the *Morning Bugle*, so if there is a reporter outside we know he comes from that paper and the footmen can deal with him. Thank goodness, the public have begun to leave us alone! Do remember! Not a word." She bustled him before her to the street door.

The Great Eastern Railway omnibus stood outside pulled by its two enormous horses. In front stood Lady Bywater's carriage. Mackintosh yapped and danced on his leash with excitement but he would not go to Marjorie, opting to travel with the servants instead.

Lord Philip stood miserably on the pavement, still hatless. The last he saw of Marjorie was her averted face.

He walked sadly home, wondering what to do. He was to wonder even more when he found Hermione and her parents, Colonel and Mrs. Ffofington, waiting for him.

In vain did he deny that he had made any

formal offer of marriage to Hermione. "It doesn't matter anyway," said Hermione bitterly. "He's just proposed to Marjorie."

The Colonel's choleric eyes flew to Lord Philip's face. "Is this true?" he demanded.

"Of course not," said Philip with a light laugh. "I only said that to tease Hermione and get a bit of my own back because she has put me in such an impossible situation." He gave Hermione a warm smile that melted her bones. "Come, Hermione, you know me better than anyone. *Would* I propose to Marjorie? Now, would I?"

"No, Philip, of course not," said Hermione with a relieved laugh. "You are such a tease."

"You naughty young things!" said the Colonel, wagging an indulgent finger. "I know you and Hermione want your fling but we shall expect to see you engaged this year, you know."

Philip smiled warmly but did not commit himself.

Hermione knew his hand must not be forced so she quickly changed the subject. "Where has dreary Marjorie gone to?" she asked.

"A place called Sandypoint, I think," said Philip. "But it's all deadly secret. Lady Bywater has made all the papers with the exception of the *Morning Bugle* agree not to print anything about her whereabouts."

"Sorry you had that bit of embarrassment,"

mumbled the Colonel. "But gels of that class can't take a joke."

"Quite," said Philip while his mind plotted and planned how to get hold of Marjorie. He had always got what he wanted. Never in his life had he been thwarted before.

Mrs. Ffofington rose to her feet, saying, "We'll leave you two young things together. It is teatime, after all." Tea time was about the only time a gentleman could be alone with a lady, unchaperoned.

Lord Philip wanted rid of Hermione as soon as possible so when her parents had left, he smiled at her in a conspiratorial way and said, "My head aches like the devil, Hermione. Do you mind trotting along. I'll see you later."

Hermione pouted. "Why didn't you say so before? I could have left with mummy and daddy."

"Because I wanted to do this," he said pulling her into his arms. He kissed her very passionately and Hermione looked up at him with a blind, shaken expression on her face.

"That should keep her quiet for a while," thought Philip.

"Philip, darling . . ." Hermione began but the door opened and the Marquess of Herterford walked in. Hermione disliked Philip's brother even more than he disliked her. So she shook out her skirts in a brisk way and picked up her reticule.

"Hallo, Robert," she cooed. "I was just leaving. Bye-bye, Philip. I'll see myself out."

Hermione shut the door firmly behind her and paused in the hall and stared at herself in the mirror. Philip was a poppet. And he loved her or he would never have kissed her like that. She straightened her hat and fished a packet of *papier poudré* from her reticule, tore off a leaf and began to powder her nose.

The deep tones of the Marquess of Herterford's voice carried through the closed door and out into the hallway with dreadful clarity.

"I just met old Lady Bywater," he said. "She had just been seeing Mrs. Wilton and Marjorie off at the station. She plans to follow them tomorrow. But that is not the point. She told me that you had offered for Miss Montmorency-James. Can't you leave the girl alone?"

"It was the only thing I could do," said Philip in a low voice. But Hermione heard what he said for her ear was now jammed to the drawing room door. "Everyone's treating me like some sort of monster. Seemed the decent thing to do."

"Can't take your medicine, eh?" said the Marquess in a lazy voice. "I hope she refused you but I suppose there's not much hope of that."

"As a matter of fact she did," Hermione heard Philip reply.

"Well what are you moping for then?" remarked the Marquess with heartless cheerfulness. "You didn't really want her anyway."

Hermione pressed closer to the door and just caught Philip's muttered, "I love her," and the Marquess's answering, "Oh, my god. You fool!"

Hermione walked very stiffly to the street door and opened it oh so quietly and closed it oh so quietly behind her. She felt as if a sudden movement, a sudden noise would break her in two. She walked all the way from Park Lane to Eaton Square, oblivious to the sights and sounds around her. She had cried once today. She did not want to cry again. Gradually her misery was alleviated by a pure burst of hate for Marjorie Montmorency-James. If she, Hermione, could find out where those damned anarchists were hiding then she would gladly give them Marjorie's direction.

But if the whole of Scotland Yard couldn't find them, then how could she?

She walked into the hallway of her home and stood staring at the telephone on its little cane table.

Slowly she walked forward and picked it up.

"Are you there?" she said primly to the operator. "Please get me the *Morning Bugle*, will you?"

* * *

The Duchess of Dunster's butler was an avid newsreader. He read every morning paper published and contrived to read every scrap of news throughout the day. He was, however, conscientious in his duties so it was not until evening that he opened his second-last paper, the *Morning Bugle*.

There on the front page was emblazoned a story, "Anarchists Threaten the Life of Miss Montmorency-James."

"A certain Society lady," he read, "telephoned our offices yesterday to relate the information that our heroine Miss Marjorie Montmorency-James who . . ." here followed a rehash of the whole business . . . "is now holidaying at Sandypoint to escape reprisals from the Camden Town Anarchists who as yet have not been found. 'I know they are bound to want to kill her,' our informant said. 'They must be furious with her for spoiling their plot and for having in a way caused the death of their leader.'"

The rest of the story developed into a political harangue against the Tories who allowed such nests of anarchists to go unscathed.

The butler reread the story. Funny, he thought, it's almost an encouragement to these anarchists to go and get her. Perhaps he should tell Lord Philip. But the poor young master had had enough of his troubles with them nasty papers. Better let his brother, the

Marquess, see it. If anything had to be done, then he would know what to do.

The Marquess was not at home so it was not until the following day that he found the cutting from the *Morning Bugle,* lying with his morning post.

He read it quickly and then swore savagely. He was sure the "Society Lady" was Hermione. He wanted to shake that girl until her teeth rattled.

He sighed. He knew where his duty lay. He must travel to Sandypoint and tell Mrs. Wilton about the article. It was more than likely she had not seen it. Surely the anarchists would not dare come near Marjorie. She had given exact descriptions of them to the police. But there was a chance that they might. It was no use consulting Philip. He would simply dash off and propose again and the girl had said she didn't want him.

In another part of London, Toby Anstruther was staring at the same article, which had reached him in almost the same way, although in this case it was his housemaid who read the *Morning Bugle* and not his butler.

He frowned. He remembered Marjorie at the river party and how she had dazzled him and made him laugh. He had thought her very silly after the poetry reading and had lost interest in her. But now he could not quite get her out of his mind. She was never boring. Perhaps some sea air was just what he needed . . .

And in a quarter of London called Limehouse, what was left of the Camden Town Anarchists sat in a small room above an opium den and stared down at a tattered copy of the *Morning Bugle*.

Phyllis and Joseph were all that was left. Charlie and Bernie and Jim had fled to Germany to try to find work in the shipyards.

Phyllis mourned Tony's death. She hated Marjorie with a terrible savagery. Marjorie in Belgravia was one thing. But Marjorie in some small seaside town was more accessible.

"Let it be," said Joseph wearily. "I'm tired of running and we'll only come unstuck again. Look at that bomb! Days of work and then it turns out that shyster sold me blacking instead of dynamite."

"You should have tried it out first," snapped Phyllis obtusely.

"What! And blown us from here to kingdom come! Have a bit of sense. I'm not going anyway."

"Well, I am," said Phyllis. "You've got to get me money."

"How?"

"In the usual way, eejit," grated Phyllis. "Go and rob someplace."

"Like where?"

"Like this dump."

"Now I know you're mad. We'd be the first

persons that heathen would think of. I don't want a lot of Chinamen wrapping me up in piano wire and dropping me in the river."

"Get it anyhows," ordered Phyllis. "I need to get clothes for a disguise and I need forged references. You know where to get *those*."

"Usual place," replied Joseph gloomily. He wished he had left with the others but he was afraid of Phyllis.

"All right," he said getting to his feet. "I'll do it. What kind of references was you wanting?"

"Servant. Housemaid. Nothing grand. I wouldn't know the work."

"Righty-ho!" said Joseph. His face looked strangely naked as he had shaved off his beard and had had his hair cropped by Phillis into a short military cut. "And if I do this for you, you'll leave me alone?" Joseph demanded.

"Course," snorted Phyllis. Joseph left feeling happier than he had done for days. He would not have felt at all happy had he realized the plans Phyllis had for him.

General Hammer was happily boring a friend of his in the middle of platform 9 at Liverpool Street Station. The friend was shuffling from foot to foot. General Hammer became more boring with the passing of the years, he thought. Just then the General ended his usual diatribe against Women's Suffrage to point to a young soldier who was trailing along the platform in the wake of a dowdy-looking maid.

"See that poor fellow?" he said. "See how sad and miserable he looks? Know why? 'Cos no one respects him, that's what. That's the trouble with this country. Anarchists running all over the place, trying to kill the King and that poor blighter is treated like mud. And know why? Heh? Heh? I'll tell you why, it's because there isn't a war on . . ."

The guard waved his flag and the General's friend thankfully escaped.

The soldier, still miserable, shrank into the corner of a third-class compartment and mumbled, "You said I didn't need to come, Phyllis."

The maid grinned at him. "Bit o'sea air'll do you good," she said. "Nothing like it!"

Chapter Seven

Sandypoint had managed to miss the vulgar boom in seaside holidays that had desecrated—in its staid opinion—so many other towns like Scarborough and Blackpool. It had its Royal Hotel complete with *thé dansant* and resident gigolo, it had its Pierrot show at the end of the pier and its donkeys on the beach. But it did not supply cheap accommodation or encourage day trippers or crowd its sedate promenade with fairground sideshows.

Gentility was the keynote and its population of elderly ladies and gentlemen was determined to keep it that way.

Mrs. Wilton had rented the same villa as she had always done. It was a large trim house with gabled windows set back from the cliff road behind a neat garden.

One had only to walk a little way down the cliff road to come to the promenade with its row of shops on one side and the neat stretch of sand lined with bathing machines on the other. In fact that *was* Sandypoint. It was a very small town. Life revolved around the elderly inhabitants of the other villas that were situated at either end of the promenade. The whole town was built in a large cove with steep cliffs rising on either side.

Mrs. Jenkins and Mrs. Bassett of Haddon Common were in residence. Mrs. Fyfe-Bartholomew had died comfortably of old age and Lady Bethons had gone to Scarborough.

Mrs. Wilton found her circle of card-playing friends expanding. It was one thing to be plain Mrs. Wilton. It was another to be Mrs. Wilton with Lady Bywater in residence.

Marjorie saw little of her grandmother and Lady Bywater. They were always out at some house or another. She was not sorry. Her grandmother looked at her so sadly and reproachfully and made Marjorie feel guilty. Marjorie knew her grandmother had put out a vast amount of money on that London Season but she, Marjorie, had failed to marry and had instead become notorious.

Her life during the first week was very dull and she set herself to woo Mackintosh away from the butler so that she might have a companion on her walks.

Mackintosh at first treated all her overtures with crusty Scottish reserve. But there was no Duke of Clarence to go to and he enjoyed running on the beach and terrifying the waves and so he gradually became used to going out with his mistress. Marjorie grew very fond of the Scottie but Mackintosh still reserved all his love and affection for the butler and would leave her immediately after one of these walks and head off to the butler's pantry, barking joyfully.

The weather continued gray and unseasonably cold and the beach was deserted, lapped by little chilly waves.

Marjorie almost succeeded in blotting out the memory of her London Season. Her mind winced away from any thought of Lord Philip.

She was sitting alone in the overstuffed drawing room of the villa, one quiet Sunday afternoon, when the Marquess of Herterford was announced.

Marjorie had one panic-stricken moment when she wished to tell Jenkins to inform my lord that she was not at home. Then she remembered she had not thanked the Marquess for his defense of her in court and allowed him to be admitted.

His slight family resemblance to his brother unnerved her but she masked her nervousness, ordered tea and sedately folded her hands in her lap.

"Good day, my lord," she said politely, "To what do I owe the honor of this visit?"

The Marquess surveyed her for a few moments. When he had seen her aboard the *Valiant,* she had been a pretty girl. Now she was a beautiful woman. She was wearing a white organdy dress tied at the waist with a wide blue sash. Her small head was held proudly by a stiff boned collar and her eyes were as bleak as the sea outside.

"May I sit down?"

She gave a little bow so he pulled up a chair and sat down holding his hat and cane and gloves in one hand as good form dictated. One must never leave the things with the butler or that would mean one did not know when to finish a call.

"I am concerned about you, Miss Montmorency-James," he said, fixing her with those peculiarly arresting eyes. "There had been a report in the *Morning Bugle* stating your whereabouts. A certain 'Society lady' had telephoned the information . . ."

"Hermione!" said Marjorie flatly.

"It's possible. The reason I am here is to warn you that the anarchists may try to kill you in revenge. I shall wait to see Mrs. Wilton and then perhaps if she permits, I will alert the local constabulary . . ."

"No," said Marjorie firmly. "Enough, my

lord. My grandmother has suffered enough over my stupidity. The anarchists will not dare to come here. They know that the whole of Britain is looking for them. If you persist in this matter, I must ask you to leave. If not . . . why, then . . . you may stay to tea."

"I will stay to tea," he said with a sudden smile. It did not have the charm or sweetness of Philip's smile but it was good-natured and natural and Marjorie thawed slightly toward him.

With a great effort, he kept away from the subject of the anarchists because she had told him not to discuss them and because . . . and because . . . and because, dash it all, he wanted to see her smile.

But try as he would, Marjorie listened to him with a social expression pinned on her face, her slim hands busy among the teacups.

"Why did you refuse Philip?" he asked abruptly. Marjorie took a small sip of tea and then very carefully placed her cup on the table.

"I wonder if we shall ever see the sun again, my lord. It really has been such dismal weather. Do have some plum cake. Our cook makes the best plum cake I have ever tasted."

He tried again. "Miss Montmorency-James. I am about to behave badly but I cannot bear to see you like this."

"Like what?" asked Marjorie, startled out of her icy calm.

"So lifeless. Philip is a wretch. He does love you, you know. He told me so."

"He loves me *now*," said the new mature Marjorie, "because I am something he cannot have. More tea, my lord? No? He is probably behaving like a thwarted child."

This accurate summing up of his brother's feelings irked the Marquess.

"What you say is true," he said wryly, "but a very cynical observation for a girl of your years. I liked the Marjorie I met on the boat much better."

"She is gone," said Marjorie. "I am not being anyone else at the moment, you see. Just myself. Since personal remarks seem to be the order of the day, my lord, may I ask if you are or have been married? When I was studying Burke's *Peerage* in my besotted way, I read only the details on Lord Philip. Not on yourself."

"Yes, I will have more tea after all. And yes, I was married. She died some ten years ago. Diphtheria."

"How sad," said Marjorie, pouring tea with a steady hand.

"How long do you plan to stay here?"

"For the rest of the summer, I suppose," said Marjorie, studying an angel cake as if it were the most fascinating thing she had ever seen.

He looked down at her bent head and despite himself found himself saying, "Your hair is very pretty, Miss Marjorie. There are little gold lights on it just where the sun is shining on it. By George! The sun!"

Marjorie stood up and walked to the window and he followed her. They stood side by side, looking out at the sea.

The gray clouds had parted and a shaft of sun was cutting down through the grayness and shining on the sea. Then, almost as they watched, a breeze sprang up, slowly stiffening into a brisk wind. Like a curtain, the clouds rolled back. The sea changed from black to gray, from gray to dull green, then from green to sparkling blue. The awnings on the bathing machines on the beach cracked in the wind and a long line of foam turned and sparkled on the golden sand.

And Marjorie turned and leaned her forehead on the rough tweed of his shoulder and cried and cried as if the sun had melted the ice in her heart. She cried with shame for all her follies, she cried for the lost innocence and trust of her adolescent emotions, she cried for that little actress, Marjorie, who had played her last and nearly fatal role.

He put his arms round her and drew her against his chest. Crying was the best thing she could do, he realized. After a long time the sobs ceased. Her lacy little handkerchief was a sodden ball. He produced a large one from his pocket and tilted up her chin and carefully dried her face.

Well, he only meant to give her a light fatherly kiss on the lips, But her mouth trembled under his and she smelled faintly of lavender water and scented soap. He was not at all aware that he was kissing her for a very long time indeed.

He was too excited and interested to discover he was experiencing a series of emotions he had never thought to experience again. Only when he tasted salt on his lips did he draw back.

Marjorie was looking at him with angry wet eyes. "Now I suppose you will apologize for your behavior and tell me it will never happen again," she said.

He looked at her curiously, still holding her in his arms.

"No," he said slowly. "I would like it to happen again. Very much."

"And then you will go away and laugh about me," sobbed Marjorie.

"There are no Hermiones in my life," he said in a husky voice. "I tell you this, Marjorie. I do not know why I did that since I do not know you very well but it was the most enchanting thing that has happened to me for a long time. The only thing I regret is the vast difference in our ages. I am thirty-seven, you know."

"That's *old!*" said Marjorie amazed.

"I suppose it is to you," he said rather sadly and Marjorie would have given the world to take that exclamation back. All of a sudden she not care *how* old he was. She did not love him, of course. She only knew that she felt at home in the circle of his arms and felt a limp, drugged feeling pervading her body and thought she might fall if he let her go.

"We shall walk, shall we?" he said softly. "In the sunshine. I must talk about these anarchists again, you know. You could be in very great danger."

Marjorie nodded dumbly and went to fetch her hat and coat. As they were walking through the hall, Mackintosh bounded through the green baize door leading from the servants' quarters with his leash in his mouth and a mutinous "I don't like you but you can take me for a walk anyway" look in his eye.

"Is that yours?" asked the Marquess.

"In a way," said Marjorie. "Mackintosh prefers the butler."

"That's the Scotch for you," mocked the Marquess, picking up Mackintosh's lease and fastening it to the dog's tartan collar, "democratic to a fault."

He held out his arm and Marjorie shyly took it. The Marquess found his brain was racing. He wanted to get her alone away from the house and kiss her again. If he went through that same gamut of emotions, then he would ask her to marry him before some other gallant came along and snapped her up.

Marjorie's thoughts were also in a turmoil. He wouldn't dare kiss her again. But then, what if he didn't want to? I must be very fast, thought Marjorie in despair. Was every man who held her in his arms going to excite passion?

She tried to remember what she had felt when Philip had kissed her and could not remember at all. She could not even remember what Philip looked like!

She glanced shyly up at the Marquess from under the brim of her hat and he immediately looked down at her and smiled.

He led her down the cliff road and along the promenade and up the cliff road at the far end until the villas petered out and the road narrowed to a path. When there was no sign of human habitation except a tiny cottage with an overstuffed front garden, he stopped and slowly drew her to him and bent his head.

"Well, if it ain't our miss," cried a voice.

The Marquess flushed and released Marjorie and both swung round. Beaming out from the roses in the cottage garden was Charlie-the-coachman. "Cor stone 'er crows," he went on cheerfully. " 'Ere's the lady wot I owe me life to, guv. Come in, come in! Got a pot o' char on the stove and you've got to see old Charlie."

"It's an old friend of mine," said Marjorie in answer to the Marquess's questioning look.

They followed Charlie around to the back of the cottage and into a tiny kitchen.

"We've had tea," said Marjorie. "But how did you come to arrive here?"

So Charlie told the story over again about Marjorie's generosity and his winnings at Ascot and reminded Marjorie she had recommended Sandypoint. A soft whicker interrupted him.

"That's Charlie-the-horse," he said. "Come along o' me. You've never seen the likes o' this."

There was a small field at the back of the house and Charlie-the-horse stood leaning dreamily against the fence. He was extremely fat and glossy and had jaunty red ribbons tied in his mane. Mackintosh barked furiously but Charlie dreamed on.

"Luverly sight, ain't it," said Charlie-the-coachman. "I reckernize your lordship from the court. Marvelous, you was."

Marjorie blushed prettily. "I didn't thank *either* of you. I wouldn't have been acquitted had it not been for both of you speaking up for me like that."

Then Charlie led them round to his front garden and pointed out every flower and plant while the Marquess listened with half an ear, wondering how soon they could get away.

At last he interrupted the catalogue with, "We must go. Miss Montmorency-James's grandmother will be wondering where she is."

"I'll just get my stick," said Charlie cheerfully, "and walk with you a little ways."

And so they were chaperoned by the elderly coachman down the path and onto the cliff road and down the cliff road and onto the promenade where he cheerfully took his leave. They were now surrounded with crowds of holidaymakers. All, it seemed, ancient with the exception of one.

" 'Ullo, 'ullo, 'ullo!" said Toby Anstruther cheerfully. "Look who's here!"

The Marquess looked at Toby's fair and foolish face and felt like punching it. Marjorie appeared to be very glad to see this monstrosity and performed the introductions prettily.

"Herterford," said Toby cheerfully. "I know your brother, Philip. Friend of his as a matter of fact. What brings you here? Keeping a paternal eye on our Miss Marjorie?"

"Merely visiting," said the Marquess coldly. He felt the gulf between his thirty-seven years and Marjorie's eighteen was growing wider and wider.

"I say," went on Toby, "I'm staying at the Royal. They're having a fancy dress ball this Saturday. Are you going by any chance, Miss Marjorie?"

"Yes," said Marjorie. "Lady Bywater is one of the patronesses."

"What are you going as? I'm dashed if I know what to wear," said Toby breezily.

"Well, I don't know either," replied Marjorie. "We're to be masked you know and Lady Bywater says a regular ball gown and mask would do but Mrs. Wilton, my grandmama, you know, has bought me a magnificent gypsy costume so I shall probably wear that."

"You going, Herterford?" queried Toby.

"No," said the Marquess shortly. "I am returning to town today."

"Better make it snappy then," said Toby with hideous jollity. "Only one train and it leaves in fifteen minutes."

The Marquess resigned himself to his fate. He was too old to go hanging at the skirts of a young girl. Marjorie had not shown by word or glance that that kiss had meant anything to her at all.

The Marquess politely raised his hat and made his farewells. Marjorie stared after him in a lost kind of way. So that kiss had meant nothing after all. She thought Toby painfully young and silly and wished she had not welcomed him so warmly.

He chattered happily at her side all the way home until she had a splitting headache. The lonely wail of the train whistle sounded over the cliffs. Marjorie felt a real feeling of sadness well up inside her. Perhaps she would have to settle for someone like Toby. Other girls seemed to. Perhaps people only fell in love and became married in books. Perhaps one was expected to look for tolerable manners and a good bank balance.

Marjorie at last decided to write a formal letter to the Marquess, thanking him for his concern. She said she was sorry he would not be at the fancy dress ball but she did understand that Sandypoint was too unfashionable a place to hold his interest. She wanted to send her love but dared not. What was love anyway? She put her "warmest regards," signed it, sealed it and stamped it and ran all the way to the postbox before she could change her mind.

Hermione called at the Duchess of Dunster's Park Lane mansion in the hopes of finding Philip at home. The butler ushered her into the drawing room and then returned a few minutes later to say that Lord Philip had gone to Benham's Costumiers in Knightsbridge. Hermione, who had been standing by the writing desk, had noticed a letter lying open with "Sandypoint" written at the top. She told the butler she would just borrow some writing material to leave a note for Philip and then waited impatiently until he had left the room.

She seized the letter. It was from Toby Anstruther. Toby had felt secure in his pursuit of Marjorie. He had heard on the society grapevine before he left London that Philip had been turned down by Marjorie. He did not, as far as he knew, plan to marry the girl but he did not want any competition around while he was having fun. He obviously considered Philip out of the running, otherwise he would not have written.

"Dear Philip," Hermione read. "Here I am in this stagnant seaside resort. It has its compensations, of course. Pretty Miss M-J. is here! We are attending a costume ball on Saturday. Miss M-J. is going as a gypsy and I plan to surprise her by turning up as the gypsy baron! See what wild antics we can get up to down here? Glad you're NOT here if you know what I mean, Yours, Toby. P.S. We are to go *masked*. I hope there are no other gypsy girls there or I might land in trouble!"

Hermione put the letter back on the desk exactly where she had found it. She must go. Philip had been enamored of girls before but she had managed to prize him away from them. She must plan. She walked away from the house with quick worried steps and was nearly run over by Amy Featherington who came wobbling up on the pavement on her bicycle. "What are you looking so worried about?" panted Amy. She never wasted baby talk on her own sex.

"Philip!" snapped Hermione, too cross to keep her news secret. She told Amy about Toby's letter while Amy's eyes grew rounder and rounder. "What will you do?" asked Amy when Hermione had finished.

Hermione bit her lip. Already, she was regretting having told Amy. "Oh, nothing," she said airily. "Toodle-oo."

She walked off quickly, leaving Amy staring after her deep in thought. A masked gypsy, thought Amy. Now *that* had infinite possibilities!

The day before the ball, Lady Bywater arrived home with Mrs. Wilton, both ladies perspiring in the heat. It transpired they had been calling on Mrs. Bassett.

"A most uncomfortable time we had of it," said Lady Bywater, unpinning her hat. "Mrs. Bassett has a new housemaid, a slatternly creature who smells quite abominably. I told Mrs. Bassett to get rid of her but Mrs. Bassett, *I* think, is too frightened of the girl to say boo! One should never let servants get the upper hand. Also this girl has a caller who is always hanging about the kitchen door, some ragtag of a fellow in shabby uniform. No regiment *I* recognize. Offered to fire the girl for her and poor Mrs. Bassett turned quite pale. Dear me.

"The ball seems to be arranged pretty well. We have the band and we have the flowers. I don't think you should go as a gypsy, Marjorie. People *always* go as gypsies or pirates or highwaymen. Now when I was a gel of your age, I went as Cleopatra—very dashing. I sent to London for the costume and it should be here today, black wig and all. Of course, I am taller than you but Stavely is a marvel with a needle. What do you say?"

Marjorie, who had been curled up on the window seat with a book, put it down with a sigh. She nodded. She did not care what she went as.

There was no fun anymore in trying to be anyone else. There was no fun either in being Marjorie.

Robert, Marquess of Herterford, stared gloomily out of the window of White's. The new glass sparkled in the hot sun. The whole of London baked and sweltered under the sun. "I wonder if we shall ever see the sun again," Miss Montmorency-James had said. Well, she was no doubt seeing it now, strolling on the arm of that chattering fool, Toby Anstruther. And he hadn't warned her properly about the anarchists.

A fancy dress ball. It made him old to think of it. The last one he had attended had been when he was twenty-five. It had been a splendid costume, especially tailored for him and he still had it.

The heat was suffocating. The sun glared through the perpetual haze of smoke that hung over London. The streets smelled terribly of horse and drains.

He needed to get out of town, didn't he? He owed it to himself.

And she had written to him, hadn't she? And sent her "warmest regards."

Chapter Eight

Toby Anstruther tied a scarlet bandana around his waist with fumbling fingers. He had drunk too much, sitting on the hotel terrace in the hot afternoon sun. He should have gone to sleep before the ball but he'd met some jolly chaps in the bar. Lady Bywater had imported the youth of the local county for the occasion, afraid that there would be no one on the floor but elderly people like herself.

He had forgotten to buy anything to stain his face and used his shoe polish instead. He applied a cork moustache with shaky fingers. He felt absolutely dreadful. Toby stumbled over to the dressing table and shook his silver flask, which gave back a reassuring glug-glug. He sighed with relief and tipped some

whiskey down his throat. Ah, that was better! Marvelous stuff. He swaggered in front of
the looking glass. *Now* for Miss Montmorency-
James!

Along the corridor, Lord Philip was also
looking at himself in the looking glass. He
thought he made a very convincing gypsy. He
had seen Toby in the bar on his arrival and
had crept quietly past. Once he put his mask
on, Toby would not even know he was at the
ball.

Downstairs in the ballroom, Marjorie was
already circling around the floor in the arms
of an elderly Major. She made a striking-
looking Cleopatra in a black-and-gold robe,
heavy black wig and black-and-gold mask.
She was glad she had not come as a gypsy.
There were at least two girls in the ballroom
dressed as gypsies.

A full moon rode above the sea outside the
long windows of the ballroom, which overlooked the terraced gardens, fronting the hotel.

Lady Bywater made a rather modern, rather
elderly Queen Elizabeth and Mrs. Wilton had
come as herself.

Marjorie easily recognized Toby Anstruther
by his fair hair. She had not told him of her
change of costume and now she was glad.

She realized that she was still hoping the
Marquess might come. It was inconceivable.
But he might.

Then she recognized Philip, although, like

everyone else, he was masked. There was no mistaking that tawny hair, those glinting blue eyes behind the mask. She looked across the room at him and felt nothing. Not a thing. He was dancing with one of the gypsy girls, switching that smile of his on like a lantern.

There was a little stir at the entrance and she looked over. One of the most magnificently costumed of the guests had arrived. He was dressed in Georgian dress, a magnificent figure from his powdered hair to his buckled shoes. His blue brocaded coat was tailored to fit his broad shoulders and his silk knee breeches and clocked stockings hugged a pair of muscular legs. Marjorie was sure that the sapphires that blazed on the lace at his throat and on his long fingers were real. His blue velvet mask only covered his eyes. There was a ripple of appreciative applause and he bowed with a tremendous flourish.

The sugar-sweet strains of the *Merry Widow* waltz started up and the Georgian gentleman turned and looked around the room. He stared for a long time at the two gypsy girls and then at the rest of the guests. His eyes fastened on Cleopatra and seemed to narrow slightly. Then he walked swiftly across the ballroom floor and bowed low before Marjorie.

"This dance is mine, my Queen," he said.

Marjorie drifted into his arms in an uninterested kind of way. She did not care how

marvelous he looked or how well he danced.
The Marquess had not come.

After a few minutes of silence, he said,
"Will my Queen of the Nile not look up at
me?"

Marjorie looked up quickly in surprise. Then
she caught her breath. She recognized those
strange golden eyes smiling at her so warmly
through the slits of the mask.

"Robert!" she gasped. "I mean . . . my lord."

"Robert," he said. "Please say Robert."

"Do you know it's me?" asked Marjorie
inanely.

"Yes, Miss Marjorie. Even with a black wig
on and your face covered up, I would know
you anywhere. I trust Cleopatra does not
have anything so anachronistic as a dance
card?"

"No. Lady Bywater did not think it a good
idea. There are so many elderly married couples who prefer to dance together."

"As we shall dance together," he said, laughing down at her surprised eyes. "I must look
after you. There may be anarchists lurking
among the guests. There are at least two
gypsy barons who, I feel sure, are at this
moment making terrible mistakes."

"You mean . . ." began Marjorie, staring
wide-eyed in the direction of Philip who was
holding one of the gypsy girls closer than the
proprieties allowed.

"Do you mind?"

"No. No, not any more. No, I don't mind in the slightest."

He swept her into the center of the floor and Marjorie turned and swayed in his arms, her happy mind shutting out past and future. The tinny sound of the town band sounded like the harps of angels.

Lord Philip was feeling elated and happy. He had Marjorie in his arms and she seemed content to stay there. She felt familiar and *right* somehow. She even sounded a little like Hermione, which made him feel more at ease. He longed for the unmasking. She was so bedecked with shawls and gold coins that he could hardly see the outline of her figure. Her hair was covered with a scarlet scarf and her large mask hid her face and only showed a glint of her eyes. He thought it would be marvelous to kiss her again. He thought how marvelous it would be to be in favor with the British public again. He suddenly could not wait. He held her even closer and whispered, "Will you marry me, my gypsy princess?"

"Oh, yes," she breathed and he heaved a sigh of relief.

In another part of the ballroom, Toby Anstruther was enjoying a tremendous joke. He thought Marjorie was a superb little actress. Why, she played the part of Amy Featherington to perfection. He felt very happy and elated. He suddenly and drunkenly envisaged a jolly life with Marjorie who could become any woman she fancied at the drop of a hat. By Jove, he would ask her to marry him.

And he did!

'Oooh, *yeth,* darling," said the gypsy girl in his arms.

The tinny orchestra struck a crashing chord and Lady Bywater climbed onto the rostrum in front of the band.

"My lords, ladies . . . and Marjorie, where *is* Marjorie? Anyway, my lords, ladies and gentlemen, the time has come to unmask!"

With sighs of relief from the elderly who had found their masks too hot and giggles and cheers from the young people, strings were untied and faces laid bare.

Philip looked down at Hermione.

Toby looked at Amy.

Hermione tugged Philip to the rostrum. He was too dazed to think or do anything but follow her. Hermione spoke quickly to Lady Bywater who held up her hands for silence.

"Happy news," she cried. "Miss Hermione Ffofington has just become engaged to Lord Philip Cavendish!"

There was a burst of applause. The drummer performed a roll on the drums. Lord Philip should have been wearing his brother's costume. He looked just like an aristocrat waiting for the guillotine to fall.

"Me too! Me too!" screamed Amy, pulling Toby with her. Amy had forgotten all about

Lord Philip. Pretty as she was, her suitors did not seem to stay around for long and now Toby Anstruther had actually proposed to her.

Lady Bywater made that announcement, reflecting to herself that both gentlemen looked very pale under their swarthy makeup. "Hermione, where *is* Marjorie?" demanded Lady Bywater.

"Yes," echoed Lord Philip in a hollow voice. "Where *is* Marjorie?"

Miss Marjorie Montmorency-James was in a dark patch of the gardens of the Royal Hotel being ruthlessly kissed by the Marquess of Herterford. "Tell Me Pretty Maiden, Are There Any More at Home Like You" played the orchestra, distance lending enchantment to its tiny strings.

The moon swung dizzily above and the dark corner of the garden smelled of warm pine. Marjorie had been trying to speak for some time but the Marquess could at times be as self-centered as his brother and his whole being was concentrated on kissing Marjorie. She was not wearing stays under her loose costume and her body seemed to melt into his. She would have spoken in the moment that he raised his head but she looked infinitely seductive with her lips parted. He quickly bent his head again and gave himself entirely up to the pleasurable sensations of exploring her mouth.

His deft long fingers opened the neck of her costume and his hands slid over her breasts. He thought he would go mad with desire and Marjorie thought she would go mad with shame. No gentleman should go this far with a lady unless . . . unless . . . unless he thought she was a woman of easy virtue.

"Robert!" she wailed in despair, pulling at his powdered hair.

"My heart?"

"How can you treat me so?" said Marjorie beginning to sob. "It's *indecent!*"

"Only," pointed out the Marquess in a practical voice, "if we weren't about to be married as quickly as possible. Which we are. Aren't we?" He gave her a little shake. She was now staring at him in a dazed way.

He pulled her into the moonlight and looked down intensely into her eyes. "Or do you think me too old for you, Marjorie? Do you?"

"Oh, no," said Marjorie, beginning to sob this time with sheer relief. "Oh, no, Robert. You're not old at all. It's just that you frightened me. I am not used to such intimate caresses. In fact, I am not used to any caresses whatever."

"Good," he muttered thickly, pulling her back into the shadows.

In no time at all Miss Montmorency-James and the Marquess of Herterford were thrashing around the pine needles in a fever of passion.

"No," he said suddenly. "Not here. I want you and a nice comfortable bed and a room with a locked door all night long. I refuse to deflower you in the damp and prickly gardens of the Royal Hotel, Sandypoint. Furthermore, Lady Bywater and Mrs. Wilton will think the anarchists have got you. We shall be little ladies and gentlemen and very restrained. I shall kiss you here . .. and here . . . and here . . . and then I shall fasten these little buttons *so* and we shall go and amaze everyone by announcing our engagement. But of course there would be no harm in just kissing you a little more . . . like this . . . and . . . this . . . and this."

"Oh, Robert, I do love you so," gasped Marjorie when she could.

"You'd better," he laughed.

"Except," went on Marjorie, "you look so strange with your white hair and costume, I hardly recognize you."

"Then I had better remind you what I *feel* like," he mocked, covering her mouth with his own. After five minutes of absorbed occupation, he added, "What about you, Marjorie? Perhaps I shall become addicted to women with black hair. No, don't take your wig off. We have to go back. Your grandmother must be fretting herself to flinders. Hold out your left hand, Marjorie."

He drew a large sapphire ring from his finger. "This was my great-great-great-grand-father's," he said, sliding it on her finger. "He was a tremendous dilettante. It is a little loose but it will do until I buy you one of your own."

"Marjorie!" came a shout from the terrace.

"There you are!" he said. "What did I tell you? Let us go in quickly."

Lady Bywater and Mrs. Wilton faced the happy couple as they mounted the steps of the terrace to the ballroom. Mrs. Wilton's sharp eyes focused on the fact that Marjorie's wig was askew, that her mouth was swollen, and that there were pine needles, leaves and twigs sticking to her costume.

Mrs. Wilton closed her eyes and said bitter-ly, "What role are you playing now, Marjorie? Harlot?"

"She is playing the role of my fiancée," said the Marquess.

"It's Herterford," said Lady Bywater glee-fully and slapped Mrs. Wilton on the back. "You owe me a monkey," she chortled glee-fully. "I bet you she'd marry a lord in the end."

"Is this true?" demanded Mrs. Wilton.

"Oh, yes!" cried Marjorie, her eyes shining.

"Pay up! Pay up!" cried Lady Bywater happily.

Mrs. Wilton stood for a moment, looking

for all the world like Queen Victoria not being amused about something.

"Bet you a monkey they have a quiet wedding!" she said suddenly to Lady Bywater.

"Done! But you'll lose again," said Lady Bywater. "They won't have a quiet wedding! Look at his face! He wants the whole world to know about it."

"No, a quiet wedding," said Mrs. Wilton firmly.

Lady Bywater shrugged. "Well, if you want to lose your money . . ."

The Marquess and Marjorie moved off, leaving the two old ladies squabbling.

"What a pair of inveterate gamblers," said the Marquess in awe. "Your grandmother will have no money left at all if she goes on in this fashion. She can't go about throwing away five hundred pounds at a time like a Regency rake."

"She wins as much as she loses," explained Marjorie. "Do we have to go back to the ballroom? I don't want to spoil anything by meeting Hermione . . . or . . . or Philip."

"You need not meet them," he said gently. "We will dance until Lady Bywater announces our engagement and then we will leave."

It was not as bad as Marjorie had expected. Lord Philip had apparently resigned himself to his fate and not for the world would he allow himself to show his hurt to the company.

He heard the announcement of his brother's engagement with a rather set face, drank a lot of champagne and soon began to feel better. He had not really wanted her anyway, he told himself. She was rather a silly little girl and he was surprised at Robert wishing to marry a person of that class. As for Toby Anstruther, he was fast alseep in a corner behind a potted palm. Amy looked down at him with a determined look on her little face. He most certainly wasn't going to be allowed to forget his proposal in the morning. Anyway she had telephoned an announcement of their engagement to all the newspapers.

Well away from the festivity of the ball in Mrs. Bassett's quiet villa, the housemaid silently opened the kitchen door and crept out into the night. What had happened to Joseph? Tomorrow was her first day off and they had planned to meet that night to discuss how to waylay Marjorie on one of her walks. But the back garden was silent, drenched in moonlight. Phyllis turned back. It was then she saw a note pinned to the kitchen door. She tore it down and took it into the kitchen to read it.

"Dere Phyllis," she read, "I cant take no more. I'm going to try and get out the country and join the others. I dont want to murder nobodys. I thinks you're mad. Joseph."

She crushed the note in her fingers, a murderous rage boiling up inside her. She and

Tony had been the only true anarchists. She alone was left to avenge his death.

The door opened and Mrs. Bassett stood there in her nightgown and curlpapers. "What are you doing standing here wasting gas?" she quavered.

Phyllis shot her employer a malevolent look. "Just off to bed," she muttered. "And don't go forgetting tomorrow's me day off."

"I won't forget," said Mrs. Bassett who was terrified of Phyllis and who had been looking forward to the maid's day off almost as much as Phyllis herself.

"Not that there's much to do in this dump," complained Phyllis.

"You could try some sea-bathing," snapped Mrs. Bassett, "although I gather you don't like water."

"I suppose that young friend o' yourn, Miss Montmorency-James goes swimmin' every day," sneered Phyllis.

Mrs. Bassett backed away before the venom in her face. "Well, no," she said. "Marjorie can't swim although I believe she is going for a dip tomorrow." Mrs. Bassett retreated hurriedly and closed the door.

She really must find the courage to dismiss this horrible maid. Perhaps she had better let Lady Bywater do it for her.

The Marquess held Marjorie very tightly

in his arms. Mrs. Wilton had allowed them ten minutes alone to say goodnight.

He gently kissed her eyelids, the tip of her nose and then her mouth. As last he reluctantly dragged his lips free. "I shall be back tomorrow evening," he said caressingly. "Please be careful. Don't let any anarchists harm you."

Marjorie shook her head and smiled mistily. Nothing could harm her now.

Chapter Nine

Next day dawned as hot and beautiful as the last. Charlie-the-coachman decided to take an early morning stroll along the promenade.

The flags in front of the Royal Hotel cracked and snapped in a fresh warm breeze and the sun warmed his tired old bones. If it was like yesterday, he thought, looking at the sky, then the breeze would soon die down and the day would be too hot to do any work in the garden. He would go back and give Charlie-the-horse his oats and a few carrots and then he would join his newfound cronies in the cool dark of the Prince of Wales taproom.

He turned to go back. A slatternly housemaid walked past him. Her face was working and she was muttering to herself.

"Stark raving mad," thought Charlie. "Some employers do 'ave 'em."

He strolled on up the cliff road and was nearing his garden gate when it hit him like a hammer blow. He had seen that face before!

But where? *Where?* That face meant danger. Somewhere in his long life on the London streets, he had seen that face. He leaned against his garden gate and thought hard.

Marjorie wondered what Robert would think if he could see her in her new bathing dress. Probably, a freak. She felt very strange and awkward. Her bathing costume consisted of a short serge dress with trousers that were tight fitting at the knees. It was made of navy serge with a white braid decoration, and felt very heavy and warm. As Charlie had predicted, the breeze had dropped and the sea was as calm as glass.

Marjorie had decided to sit on some flat rocks at the end of the beach near the villa and splash her feet in the water. She had decided against hiring one of the bathing machines since it was nearly noon and unless one hired a bathing machine early in the morning, it could be rather an uncomfortable experience. It was ill-lit, ill-ventilated and the floor was usually covered with sand and water from the previous occupants. Also one had to change while the machine was set in motion, a most undignified process trying to don a bathing dress while the bathing machine shook and jolted its way down to the water.

Accompanied by Mackintosh, she descended the cliff road, wearing only a long housedress over her costume. Feeling rather shy, although there was no one around, most of the holiday-makers being on the sandy beach some distance away below the promenade, she undressed and sat down on a smooth rock and let her feet slide into the cool water. She had no intention of getting her bathing suit wet. She could not swim and the water seemed very deep.

She studied little silver fish darting in the clear depths and thought about Robert.

Faint sounds of laughter came from the promenade. A Punch and Judy show was in progress and she could hear the shrill squeaks of Punch. Far out at sea, a yacht idled with limp sails, "as idle as a painted ship, upon a painted ocean."

Marjorie could hardly believe her luck. She was in love. She was loved and she would see him again that very evening.

The sun was very hot on her head and she realized she had better open her parasol or her skin would be absolutely ruined.

She drew her feet out of the water and stood up and walked a little way to pick up the large Japanese parasol she had brought with her. Mackintosh grabbed hold of the end of it in his teeth and tried to worry it, making happy little growling noises.

"Leave it alone, do!" cried Marjorie. "Bad dog!" But Mackintosh still held on with the pertinacity of his race. Not only Miss Montmorency-James could weave fantasies. Small dogs enjoyed them as well. To Mackintosh, the end of the parasol was a mortal enemy and it was his duty to savage the beast.

Both dog and mistress were so engrossed in their tug-of-war that they did not notice the housemaid who stood quite close to them. Marjorie did not notice until it was too late.

Something made her look up.

"Phyllis!" she gasped.

Phyllis lunged and gave her an almighty shove and Marjorie catapulted dack into the water. "Sink, you bitch!" cried Phyllis jumping up and down in her rage. *"Drown!"*

With a roar, Mackintosh dropped the parasol and rushed at Phyllis. He grabbed a handful of her skirt and tore. Phyllis seized the parasol and raised it to beat him off when she heard loud cries from the promenade.

"Anarchist! Murderer! Where? Where?"

Phyllis did not wait to see the end of Marjorie Montmorency-James. She started up the path, up the cliff road, and cried out in dismay. Three of the local constabulary were on their way down to the beach from Marjorie's summer home. For Charlie-the-coachman had remembered. He had remembered seeing that face poking up from the area steps in Gospel Oak. He had saddled up old Charlie and ridden the fat old horse hell for leather to the police station, shouting at the top of his voice, "The anarchists are in town! The anarchists are in town!" like some modern-day Paul Revere.

Phyllis turned and ran with two of the policemen at her heels. The third ran to rescue Marjorie. Mackintosh had forgotten about her, he had even forgotten about his drowning mistress as he happily lay in the sun and chivvied the piece of Phyllis's skirt he had torn loose.

Fortunately for Phyllis, the constabulary of Sandypoint were not given to much action and she might have escaped had it not been for the elderly holidaymakers of the resort.

Charlie's story had spread around the town like wildfire. A group of elderly residents had been holding a meeting on the promenade to protest the installation of slot machines that portrayed moving pictures and were little better than a peep show, in their opinion. One was actually called "The Romping Girls on the Swing" and portrayed a vastly indecent show of ankle and even *calf*. Horrors! They were hard at it when Charlie's story hit them, and at the same time, they heard the police whistles and saw the fleeing figure of Phyllis heading toward them.

Now Phyllis to them was the personification of every evil that had come to plague the dignity of their declining years, from motor cars to Bolshevists. They spread out, about twenty of them, across the promenade to block her way.

Phyllis screamed and tore and battled and clawed her way through. It was like some elderly hell. Toothless gums mouthed at her, parasols with iron spokes that had seen Queen Victoria's coronation came down on her head and back, withered hands clawed at her face, feeble old voices grown strong with hate cursed her in return.

She escaped them and ran headlong toward the station. Far away over the cliff came the whistle of the arriving train.

Undeterred, the rejuvenated elderly posse scampered after her. More elderly residents tottered from their houses to try to bar her way. The sun blazed down and she was bleeding and panting and nearly demented. She fled onto the station platform.

And they followed her, mouthing and mumbling, clutching a terrifying assortment of weapons from walking canes to steel hatpins nearly a foot long.

Phyllis backed to the edge of the platform.

The police, who had been chasing quite the wrong lady after losing Phyllis among the melee of elderly bodies on the promenade, had found the scent again and their whistles could be heard sounding nearer up the station rise and mingling with the wailing whistle of the approaching train.

Phyllis's tormenters moved closer, rheumy old eyes alight with hate, arthritic hands stretched out. Her mind, never stable, snapped.

With one loud scream of horror, she fell backward under the wheels of the approaching train.

Her pursuers turned in the blink of an eye back into elderly lavender-scented ladies with impeccable manners and elderly retired military gentlemen, respectable grandfathers to a man.

With one accord, they turned their backs on the scene and began to make their trembling, stately way back to the promenade.

It was up to the police to clean up the mess. They were not ghouls, after all.

Apart from having thrown up a considerable amount of salt water, Marjorie had suffered no hurt. She was helped back to the villa by the sympathetic policeman. Mackintosh escaped to the kitchen to look for Jenkins the butler. His walk had not been very much fun after all. He found his mistress thoroughly disappointing and by a series of little growls and whines tried to tell Jenkins so. Lady Bywater bustled off into town to hire extra help to defend the villa against an invasion by the press.

Marjorie was pronounced strong enough to

make a statement to the local police and on the following day to Scotland Yard, whose representative had traveled down to find out if she possibly knew of the whereabouts of the remaining anarchists.

The whole story was blazoned across the front page of every newspaper. Lord Philip Cavendish could stand no more. He left the country for an extended stay abroad and not even his fiancée knew his address.

The Marquess moved his bags and baggage into the villa with the splendid excuse that Marjorie needed extra protection. After some days, the press were informed that the Marquess of Herterford and Miss Montmorency-James had left for Paris to be married by the British Consul and by the time they found that it was not true, they didn't know where to look.

The days continued, long and hot and becoming increasingly sultry. A purple haze lay at the base of the cliffs in the evening, old bones ached and bunions jumped. Rain was forecast. But it never came.

The atmosphere between the Marquess and his love became increasingly strained. Arrangements for a wedding were postponed until the furor should die down. Anywhere they put up the bans would be sure to draw the press and the populace like flies.

Mrs. Wilton and Lady Bywater held strictly to the view that men—even gentlemen like the Marquess—would slake their lusts at the first given opportunity if not properly chaperoned. The Marquess and Marjorie were always chaperoned on their walks and, in the villa, they were never alone, even for a minute.

The villa was overstaffed to say the least. There was Stavely, Lady Bywater's lady's maid, the upstairs maid and the downstairs maid and the in-between-stairs maid. There was Rose, the parlormaid, the cook, the scullery maid, the brace of footmen, Jenkins the butler and the outside help in the form of an elderly gardener and a young odd-job man and the coachman.

The Marquess felt too old to seize kisses on the stairs or behind doors. He put a tight rein on his emotions and told himself he was content to wait. Marjorie began to feel neglected. Sometimes she wondered what had happened to the rest of the anarchists. Sometimes she even found herself hoping for another attempt on her life—*anything* that would rouse Robert from his seeming apathy.

Joseph, Bernie, Charlie and Jim had finally met up in Hamburg after many vicissitudes. Work was hard to come by—the sort of work they wanted, that is. Wages were low and hours were long. Joseph and Charlie were working as waiters in a *biergarten* owned by a Herr Hoffer where they rented a room that they shared with the other two.

After Joseph and Charlie had worked long hours serving out mug after mug of beer to the jolly German bourgeoisie, they would sit in the room, far into the night, cursing the world that gave fat fools like Hoffer all the money and them, nothing at all. They never paused to consider that Herr Hoffer had worked for years to achieve his present prosperity, nor that they owed their lodgings to his kind heart in a city where there was a strange undercurrent of anti-British feeling. They wanted what he had and plotted how they could possibly get it.

It so happened that Herr Hoffer closed down his *biergarten* every year for the month of August. He took his fat jolly wife and his two fat jolly daughters off to the Harz mountains for a vacation. This year, Joseph was to be left in charge as caretaker. It was too good an opportunity to miss. Herr Hoffer had a soft spot for Joseph and Charlie. Without their beards and shaggy hair, they seemed small and white and undernourished. They always seemed to treat him with deference and they did their work well. Herr Hoffer shrugged a fat shoulder when cronies warned him about the folly of leaving a foreigner in charge of his establishment. He had a trusting nature and did not see any reason to change this late in life.

"Now, Joseph," he said as he handed over the keys, "I trust you to look after my business. No one is to be allowed into my office for any reason. I have sacks of gold in that safe, sacks of gold." Here he gave a fat chuckle and nudged Joseph in his bony ribs

Joseph nearly died of excitement. Sacks of gold! Innocent Herr Hoffer never thought for a moment that anyone could be so naïve as to believe he kept sacks of gold in his safe. It was merely a family joke that he thought Joseph shared. In fact he kept nothing but his account books and ledgers in there while he was on holiday, all money being lodged in the bank.

Joseph and Charlie went out to the front of the *biergarten* to wave the Hoffer family goodbye. But no sooner had the cumbersome traveling coach turned the corner of the street than they raced indoors and upstairs to join the other two.

Bernie and Jim listened wide-eyed to Joseph's tale of gold. "And see," said Joseph, waving a massive bunch of keys, "the old fool's left me this!"

Trembling with excitement, they headed straight for Herr Hoffer's office.

The keys were all neatly labeled. They unlocked the office and threw open the door. A large safe squatted in all its majesty in the corner. Joseph began to search diligently through the bunch of keys. There was nothing marked "safe" and the great tough steel monster had a combination dial on the front of it that seemed to wink at them in the sunlight.

"I knew it was too good to be true," groaned Charlie.

"Look here," said Joseph, "maybe we're going the wrong way about things again. I mean ter say, we've got a good billet here and the police ain't looking for us." But he eyed the safe hungrily.

"Phyllis was right," sneered Jim. "You ain't got no guts nohow. Thought you could blow things up. Can't you get some dynamite or nitro? Thought you was a peter merchant."

"Well, I ain't," snapped Joseph. "I make bombs. That's all."

"Sure you do," mocked Jim, "with cakes o' boot polish."

"We'll get nowheres fighting," said Charlie. "Let's go out after dark someplace in the town where we'll meet the right sort of person."

The right sort of person was a different "right sort" from the kind a Lady Bywater, say, would expect.

Like the criminals they were, they gravitated instinctively to other criminals, moving after dark through the cellars and bars of the meaner part of town.

At last they found what they were looking for and could hardly believe their luck. A large drunken Pole had the goods to sell, sixteen cakes of Atlas dynamite. Joseph forgot his fears and scruples. He had earlier that evening been given another reason to forget them. The *Hamburger Zietung* carried a description of Phyllis's death on the inside pages and also a description of the four remaining anarchists.

The deal being struck and the goods handed over, all Joseph had to do was construct a small kind of charge that would blow the safe. He was not quite sure how to do it but felt sure a big enough blast would do the trick.

It was a tremendous blast. It was superb! It could be heard all over Hamburg. It blew the four anarchists to kingdom come and half destroyed the *biergarten*.

The safe was completely untouched.

In a tin box in the four young men's room, papers and newspaper cuttings were found that identified the four as the missing English anarchists.

"Well, they've gone to join Phyllis wherever she might be," said the Marquess putting down his newspaper a day later. A small sulky sigh was all that greeted this bit of news. He looked at his beloved with intense irritation. The servants had been allowed the day off to go to a fair in the town; Lady Bywater and Mrs. Wilton had been unable to withstand the lure of a bridge party. They were alone for the first time, it seemed, in weeks.

The heat was suffocating and the rooms of the villa, claustrophobic. One lived in a perpetual twilight as the blinds were always drawn each morning against the glaring sun.

It was, the Marquess thought, an ideal opportunity for some dalliance. But how could he dally when his beloved sat there looking for all the world like a sulky schoolgirl? She had managed in the past few days to make him feel like a stern parent. He did not know that Marjorie had unconsciously been trying to break down his reserve, even if it meant getting him angry. She had even gone so far as to flutter her eyelashes at the brace of footmen but all *that* got her was a cold, contemptuous look.

The Marquess picked up his paper again and rattled it noisily. Marjorie thought he looked very handsome—and forbidding.

He was dressed in a Norfolk jacket, breeches and gaiters. Those strange and exciting eyes of his, which should have been looking lovingly into her own, were bent on that dreary paper. Marjorie was wearing a clinging gown of lilac *crêpe de chine*. The Marquess rattled his newspaper again and envied her cool clothes. He had forgotten, despite his extensive experience, what went under such pretty gowns.

Marjorie was wearing a straight-fronted corset that had long metal stays at the front. She was padded over the back, hips and chest to produce the effect of a seemingly miniscule waist. The corset was worn over a chemise, which was tucked into a pair of heavy silk drawers, which were lashed round the waist with tapes. Her chemise was pulled in extra tight to support her breasts. In all, the whole ensemble was about as cool as a straightjacket. Her skin prickled all over under the weight of clothes and she longed to pull the whole lot off and have a damn good scratch.

Men had a much easier time, she reflected. They didn't have to wear any of this rubbish..

The Marquess with his high hard collar torturing his neck and his long hard cuffs torturing his wrists would have thought her mad if he could have read her thoughts. And what on earth had possessed him to put on a tweed Norfolk jacket and knickerbockers in this heat?

"Let's go for a walk," said Marjorie abruptly.

"Is that all you can think about?" he asked. "We are left alone for the first time and you want to go for a walk."

"What else is there to do?" countered Marjorie, staring at the pattern in the Wilton carpet.

"Oh, if you can't think of anything else, I'm not going to tell you." He threw down his newspaper. He had been about to suggest that he go and change into a blazer and flannels but he perversely decided to stay in his tweeds and suffer.

Marjorie pinned a large shady straw hat on

her head with two large hatpins. It was decorated with a whole cornucopia of wax fruit.

In grim silence they walked down toward the promenade about three feet apart. The air was like hot soup and Marjorie was suffering from an incipient headache. Her underwear clung to her constricted body and she felt the beginnings of a heat rash beginning to spread over her skin.

Great black clouds were boiling up over the horizon, towering up into the blue sky, great black-and-purple citadels.

Anyone with any sense had gone indoors and the promenade appeared deserted, except for a workman who was removing the coins in the slot machines.

The Marquess stopped and leaned his elbows on the rail of the promenade and stared gloomily at the black sea.

"You should have brought that poor beast, Mackintosh, out for a walk," he said.

"He prefers the butler," said Marjorie in a cold little voice.

"Sensible animal."

"What's that supposed to mean?"

The Marquess turned and leaned his back against the rail. "It means," he said, "that I can understand him going to where he gets more warmth and affection than he does from you."

"Perhaps you would like to do the same?" said Marjorie. How she hated him! How could she have been silly enough to ever think she loved him. He was cold and pompous.

"Perhaps." The Marquess stared back at her with equal dislike. Silly little girl with all her stupid sulky posturing. He must have been mad.

"Ho, there folks!" Charlie-the-coachman reined in beside them. Charlie-the-horse was pulling the old growler, which had been revarnished to a high shine. "Likes to take the old wagon out for a bit," he said. "Congratulations on your engagement, miss, my lord."

"Thank you," said Marjorie bleakly, although she gave Charlie a warm smile. Charlie was always a dependable character. Bluff and cheery, the salt of the earth.

The Marquess said nothing.

Charlie looked in a worried way from one stony face to the other. He picked up the reins and stared straight between his horse's ears. "If you'll take the advice of an old man, me lord," he said, "you'll go in for a bit o' slap and tickle. Ain't nothing like it. Me and my missus—may she rest in peace—when we was engaged, it wor a bit o' a strain what with 'er Ma always on the watch. Started quarreling we did. But a bit o' slap and tickle put it right." He touched his hat and the growler moved off.

Marjorie felt her face flaming. Such impertinence! And from Charlie too! She felt just as if Santa Claus had pinched her bottom.

The Marquess looked at her in a speculative kind of way.

He opened his mouth to say something when there came an almighty crash of thunder and the heavens opened. He seized her hand and began to run. By the time they reached the villa they were soaked to the skin. The telephone in the hall was ringing away. The Marquess answered it and then turned to Marjorie.

"That was Mrs. Wilton," he said. "It seems they will not be home in time for dinner owing to the weather."

Marjorie stood awkwardly in the hall, her hat a wreck and water pouring down her face.

"Go upstairs, girl," he said, giving her a push. "We'll need to get out of these wet things."

He was just giving himself a brisk rubdown with a towel in his own room when he heard a muffled wail from Marjorie's. He quickly donned a dressing gown and walked along the corridor to her room. He opened the door without knocking.

Marjorie stood in the middle of the room, tears running down her face. She was fighting with the tapes of her corset, which had worked themselves into a Gordian knot. She was too miserable to care whether he saw her in her underwear or not.

"Turn around!" he ordered.

His long fingers seized the tapes of the corset and broke them and unlaced the rest of the tape. The heavy garment fell to the floor with an enormous clatter. He looked at it with awe and at the pile of horsehair pads attached to Marjorie. He went along to the bathroom and came back with an armful of towels and in a deft impersonal way stripped off the rest of her undergarments, deaf to her faint shrieks of protest. He rubbed her briskly with the towel, his mind registering how well he was behaving.

He flung back the covers of the bed. "In you go," he ordered, "and I'll bring you some hot tea."

He walked smartly to the door and then stopped dead, his hand on the handle.

"Robert!" came a faint voice from the bed. "I'm sorry I was such a grouch."

He slowly turned round. She was smiling at him weakly, her damp hair spread around her shoulders, the blankets up to her chin.

And then he didn't really know what had happened. Somehow he was in bed with Marjorie, he was on top of Marjorie and he was making love to her as he had never made love before while the villa rocked to the force of the storm and drowned the noises from the

storm of passion taking place in Miss Montmorency-James's bed.

"You win," muttered Lady Bywater to Mrs.
Wilton. Both old ladies were seated at a small
table in the drawing room much later that
day playing backgammon. The Marquess and
Marjorie were seated side by side on a sofa in
front of the fire.

"What do you mean 'win'?" demanded Mrs.
Wilton. "We've hardly started playing."

"I mean you win the bet about the small
wedding. They'll have to be married quickly
and quietly." She leaned forward and lowered
her voice. "Look at their faces. They've been
and gone and done it!"

And they had!